"Ellie? Ellie Owen

"I just go by Elle now,

Nice, but a total shock. Racking her brain, she remembered the last time she'd seen him— graduation. At twenty-two, Cam had not only been the older brother of the love of her life but he'd already been to college and had returned with a full beard.

The truth was that Cameron Dumont had always sort of intimidated her. Hell, he'd intimidated the whole town. He was a loner, always off in some corner. Not brooding, but watching, observing, with a self-assured confidence that no other adolescent possessed. With long hair and dark looks, he'd always seemed...dangerous, she decided. He was full of muscles and well over six feet tall.

Looking at him now, it was evident that he was still built and dangerous-looking, if not cleaned up a bit from ten years ago. Elle felt a little flutter of some kind of awareness as she took in his now beardless, square jawline, broad shoulders and arms rippling with muscles.

"Welcome home, Elle," he said. "You look...great."

* * *

SAVED BY THE BLOG: This matchmaking gossip columnist won't stop until true love wins!

Dear Reader,

I'm so excited to reveal my very first book for Harlequin Special Edition. The first romance novels I ever read were Harlequin Special Edition, and Harlequin has been a great reading companion to me over the years, providing brief respites from the everyday, lots of dreamy sighs, occasional gasps and happy endings.

I'm often asked where I get my ideas for stories. Usually, I don't remember or it's a mix of different moments and inspirations. But for this book, I was walking my dog, Harry, one day and the town of Bayside popped into my head. Just like that. I saw the entire town, the bay, Elle and Cam, The Brewside, the Dumont mansion, everything. I remember thinking, *I'd love to live there!* And so I got to for the next couple of years.

Of course, I had to add some of myself into the mix. You can find me in the name of the town. All hail my favorite television show. Just like Harlequin books, *Saved by the Bell* and Bayside High often helped me escape the day-to-day, made me laugh, smile and sometimes even cry. I hope to offer the same to you.

I hope you love *Falling for the Right Brother* and the entire Saved by the Blog series. I'd love to connect, so please visit my website at kerricarpenter.com, or find me on Facebook, Twitter and Instagram. I promise not to bombard you with too many dog pictures. Well...maybe.

Happy reading and glitter toss,

Kerri Carpenter

Facebook.com/AuthorKerri

Twitter.com/authorkerri

Instagram.com/authorkerri

Falling for the Right Brother

Kerri Carpenter

HARLEQUIN® SPECIAL EDITION®

Recycling programs
for this product may
not exist in your area.

ISBN-13: 978-0-373-62355-6

Falling for the Right Brother

Copyright © 2017 by Kerri Carpenter

Printed in U.S.A.

Award-winning romance author **Kerri Carpenter** writes contemporary romances that are sweet, sexy and sparkly. When she's not writing, Kerri enjoys reading, cooking, watching movies, taking Zumba classes, rooting for Pittsburgh sports teams and anything sparkly. Kerri lives in Northern Virginia with her adorable (and mischievous) rescued poodle mix, Harry. Visit Kerri at her website, kerricarpenter.com, on Facebook (Facebook.com/AuthorKerri,) Twitter and Instagram (@authorkerri), or subscribe to her newsletter.

For My Dad

If only everyone had a dad like mine,
the world would be a much better (and funnier) place.

Chapter One

Good morning, avid readers! Who's ready to be saved by the blog? Boy, do I have some juicy gossip that will help you escape the day-to-day life of our very small town.

Rumor has it one of Bayside's most infamous residents is returning today after a ten-year absence. You may remember this gal as lover of all things Jasper Dumont. Who can forget the time she declared her love for him by, ahem, making that little video? Haven't seen it? I'm sure someone saved a copy. *Smirk*

Personally, I'm thrilled that she's back. So with that, let me, your fabulous Bayside Blogger, be the first to say… Welcome back to Bayside, Ellie Owens.

Elle stepped off the airport tram, thanked the driver and retrieved her luggage. Inhaling a deep whiff of air, she caught the familiar salty scent she associated with home.

As the tram drove away, she stood on the stone sidewalk in the center of town, taking a moment to reacquaint herself with Bayside, Virginia. Still pleasant to look at with its town square full of eclectic shop fronts and its flower-lined streets. Tucked behind one side of the square was the bay, the heart and soul of the town. The water looked calm today as fishing boats returned to their docks after their early-morning fishing trips.

Elle knew if she squinted her eyes just right she would be able to see the small, two-bedroom bungalow she'd shared with her father until she'd turned eighteen and went off to college, and then directly on to Italy after that. One of the many things she'd missed from home was her brightly painted yellow house with its rickety deck and even more dilapidated dock that stretched out into the water. It wasn't unlike the other houses on that side of the bay.

She also knew that if she stood out on the dock, she would be able to take in the much larger and more impressive houses—mansions, really—on the other side of the water. That's where the Dumont house sat, surrounded by tactfully placed trees and discreet fences.

How many nights had she sneaked out after she was supposed to be asleep to take in the lights and music coming from that magical house? It seemed the Dumonts threw parties with the same frequency that other people went to the grocery store.

Apparently there was nothing like a Dumont party. Everyone in town had heard about the expensive champagne, live music and occasional fireworks. Although that wasn't surprising for a family who had made more money than God in real estate.

She'd heard that one time the Dumonts had hired ballroom dancers to entertain their guests. Another time they'd flown in a top chef from Japan to make fresh sushi for Mrs. Dumont. Once they'd even hired a troupe of Cirque du Soleil performers for a birthday celebration.

But out of all those special occurrences that came and went, one thing was always present. One person, actually. The person who'd taken on the role of prince of the castle in her childhood fantasies.

Jasper Dumont.

Even a shy bookworm like Elle had known of Jasper. In fact, everyone in town knew Jasper. Well liked, crazy hot, an incredible athlete in multiple sports and the most popular kid in school. No wonder Elle had harbored a huge crush on him.

When his parents had thrown their parties, she used to pretend that Jasper was dancing in a tuxedo and drinking champagne. In reality, he was probably at one of the parties in the local park drinking cheap beer with the rest of the cool kids.

She'd certainly never been invited to those parties. But Elle's dad had always said she was an old soul. And maybe she was. Maybe she wanted to be kissed on the dance floor, like they did in the old black-and-white movies as twinkly lights illuminated the scene. Maybe she'd promised herself that one day she would go to this fictional party at the Dumonts'.

The funny thing was that Elle had attended tons of parties like that when she'd moved to Italy. She'd drunk amazing sparkling wine in centuries-old piazzas. She'd danced around local vineyards and listened to phenomenal musicians while sitting on the Spanish Steps. She'd even made out in the Blue Grotto when she visited Capri. Didn't get much more romantic than that.

But that dream—that silly childhood dream—would always persist. Who forgot about their first love? Even if that first love was the exact reason why she'd had to leave her home.

The sound of a honking horn drew her attention. A tall, attractive man dressed in jeans and a T-shirt stepped out of a silver truck and walked toward her. Elle felt her eyes go wide as she realized who it was.

No way, she thought.

"Cam?" she called out with a small wave as she pushed her large sunglasses on top of her head.

He stopped midstride, smack-dab in the center of the street. She thought his mouth fell open but couldn't quite see from her angle. Cocking his head, he pushed his hands into the pockets of his worn jeans and took her in. Not until a car horn blasted did he move. Shaking his head, he waved to the driver to pass and continued toward her.

"Ellie? Ellie Owens?" he asked.

"I prefer Elle now, but yes. Nice to see you."

Nice, but a total shock. Racking her brain, she remembered the last time she'd seen him—graduation. At twenty-two, Cameron Dumont had not only been the older brother of her biggest crush, but he'd already been to college and had returned with a full beard.

The truth was that Cam had always sort of intimidated her. Hell, he'd intimidated the whole town. He was a loner, always off in some corner, watching, observing, with a self-assured confidence no other adolescent possessed. With long hair and dark looks, he'd always seemed... dangerous, she decided. He was full of muscles and well over six feet tall.

Looking at him now, it was evident that he was still tall, built and dangerous looking, if not cleaned up a bit from ten years ago. Elle felt a little flutter of some kind of awareness as she took in his square jawline, broad shoulders and arms rippling with muscles.

"Welcome home, Elle," he said. "You look...great."

The disbelief in his voice didn't surprise her. After all, the last time she'd stood in Bayside, she'd been, well, less than glamorous, that was for sure. She'd never worn makeup—her father never allowed it. And when your dad was the chief of police, you tended to listen. Her wardrobe choices hadn't been the most flattering, either—lots of jeans, flannels and sweatshirts. Total tomboy clothes. And maybe she'd carried around a little extra weight. But she'd been more into academics than athletics.

Somewhere between college and moving to Italy she'd dropped the weight, figured out how to apply makeup and let her straight brown hair grow out of the unfortunate cut she'd gotten at her dad's barbershop at the end of high school.

"Thanks," she said with a smile.

"Have you always had those dimples?"

"What?" she asked with a surprised laugh.

"Nothing. Sorry."

Searching the square, she tried to find her father's car before she realized that she had no idea what kind of vehicle he drove now.

"I just got in from the airport. I'm waiting for my dad to pick me up," she explained to Cam.

He shook his head. "Sorry, I should have said right away. Your dad called me this morning and asked if I could bring you home. Something came up." He looked away.

The reminder of why she'd returned from Italy came crashing back into her mind. "Is he at the doctor's?"

Cam nodded and quickly changed the subject. "Let me help with your bags." He grabbed all three of her bags with an exaggerated groan. "How many bodies do you have in here?"

"Just a few." Elle picked up her carry-on and purse, then followed him to his truck. She noticed that *Bayside Builders* was emblazoned on the side in black block lettering. After securing her luggage in the back, Cam surprised her by opening the passenger-side door. She slid into the truck as he skirted the hood and climbed into the driver's seat.

After starting the engine, he turned to her again. "It's been a while, Elle."

She could feel the heat flooding her cheeks. Was he referring to the night she wished she could forget? There was one particular bad memory she'd give anything to erase. "That was a long time ago, Cam," she said defensively.

Frowning, he turned in his seat to face her. "What was a long time ago?"

She rolled her eyes. "You know exactly what I'm talking about." Seeing his blank expression, she paused, then decided to get it all out in the open. "The video…about Jasper," she whispered, even though they were alone in the truck.

If she closed her eyes, she could see her dad's disappointed face as he watched his only daughter hiccup and slur as she drunkenly professed her love for Jasper Dumont.

How could she think making that video would get Jasper to notice her? Maybe because the alcohol hadn't allowed her to think at all. It definitely didn't help when her oversize T-shirt had slipped off her shoulder, giving way to a wardrobe malfunction that would have made any reality-TV star blush.

To be honest, it wasn't as though Elle had obsessed over the video every day for the last decade. Certainly not while she'd lived in Italy, the most beautiful place in the world. Why was it, then, that as soon as she stepped onto the sidewalk of her hometown the memory of the one bad thing she'd ever done came slamming back in crystal clear vision?

To her shock, Cam started laughing, his deep voice filling the truck. "Oh, my God, I forgot all about that."

What the hell? How could he act so blasé about the fateful event that almost got her suspended and laughed right out of town? Even now the thought of it could produce an embarrassed blush on her face the color of a ripe Italian tomato.

He must have noticed her doing her best blend-in-with-the-seat impression because his own expression softened. "Don't tell me that stupid little video is why you've stayed away all these years?"

Stupid? Little? No way. It had been the single most humiliating experience of her life. And while it might not have been the reason her dad had shipped her off to college in a galaxy far, far away, it hadn't helped matters.

In the end, her dad had, as usual, been right. She'd needed to get far away from Bayside—to forget, and to become her own person, without all the baggage weighing her down. Besides, she'd loved college, especially when she took a year to study abroad. Her love affair with Italy began then, and concluded after her graduation, when she'd moved to Florence for grad school. Staying in Italy for an art history major was a no-brainer. She'd been able to work in the most amazing museums and galleries. Every second she spent at the Uffizi, San Marco Museum, the Accademia or the Palazzo Vecchio had been among the most amazing moments in her life, and did help her forget. A little.

Still, she'd missed home.

"Happy to be back?" Cam asked as if he'd read her mind, before pulling out into the light traffic.

"I missed...certain things."

"Your dad," he supplied softly.

She smiled for a moment before it faded. The worry that had nestled inside her belly began to spread, causing her to roll down her window.

"How is he really?" she asked quietly.

Elle still couldn't believe her dad had kept the cancer diagnosis from her. When he'd finally told her, he'd been so flippant about it. "Oh, it's only bladder cancer. That's one of the easy ones."

There was nothing easy about cancer.

Cam followed suit and rolled his own window down. "He had some rough moments toward the end of the treatment period. But I think overall he's doing really well. Except for a couple days off here and there, he never stopped working."

For twenty-four years her dad had been the chief of

police in Bayside. After her mom had died, they'd moved back to her father's hometown for a fresh start. While he'd retired a couple years ago, no one could keep a man who'd been working since the age of ten at home. He'd been volunteering as security at the local high school ever since.

"Really?" she asked.

Cam nodded. "Sure. Heard he broke up a minor fight last week."

"A fight? Is he okay? Should he even be doing that right now?"

He slanted a steady glance in her direction. "He's fine. Don't worry. The whole town's looking out for him."

Yeah, the way they'd looked out for him ten years ago? Elle shook her head and willed the memories away. It hadn't been the town's fault he didn't get voted in as county sheriff. That had been her doing. Her and that damn video. She wiped her sweaty palms on her khaki linen pants.

Cam turned the truck onto Bay View Road, heading away from the center of town. They passed the fork in the road, the one that would take them to either the east side, known as the nice, wealthy portion of town, or to the west side, where she lived.

"Really," he added with another sidelong glance as she raised an eyebrow.

"Please tell me the truth." She could hear the urgency in her voice.

"The truth is he has cancer."

She gulped. "I gathered that part already." Typical. The very few conversations she'd ever had with Cam had been pretty similar. He hadn't been known for his words. Or his demeanor. Really, he'd been a loner. A tall, somewhat scary kind of recluse.

Elle didn't know what she was expecting now. To be honest, the fact that he was giving her a ride home was a huge step toward the socialization of the Cameron Dumont she knew.

Then he did something that surprised her. Cam reached over and squeezed her hand.

Her eyes grew wide and she inhaled sharply. If anyone ever asked, she would claim it was nothing short of shock at him being nice. The reality of the situation was that the touch of Cam's callused hand on hers made her feel…something.

"He's going to be fine," he said.

She didn't know why, but the statement made her feel better for the moment. "So," she began, searching for something to say as she reclaimed her hand and clasped it with the other one. "You're still in Bayside."

"Yep."

"Working for your parents' company?"

His hands tightened on the steering wheel. "Nah. I started my own business."

"Really?" That was a surprise. Cam was the oldest son in a four-generation family business. Naturally, he was supposed to take over the reins. "Also doing real estate?"

"Construction. I'm a contractor."

"Bayside Builders," she said, putting it together. He looked over. "I saw the name on the side of the truck."

"That's my company."

She wanted to ask more questions, but they'd reached 14 Bay View Road. Cam threw the truck into Park and slid out of his door. But Elle didn't move. Instead, she let her homesick eyes drink in the sight of the one level house she'd lived in for most of her life. It looked exactly the same, even though she could tell it wasn't. Her dad had put a fresh coat of paint on. There were new shutters and the landscaping was different.

But it was home and therefore would always be exactly what she needed to see.

"Traditionally, you leave the car when you reach your destination."

She glanced up at Cam standing in her window, watching her. Rolling her eyes, she offered him a small smile. "Good thing you're here to help me with these super hard ways of the world."

His mouth twitched before he opened her door and reached across her to unbuckle her seat belt. Elle caught a whiff of a very masculine scent. Something musky, but clean. Like a really fresh soap laced with wood.

"When did you get rid of the beard?" she couldn't help asking.

Confusion passed his face. Then he ran a hand over some appealing-looking stubble. "Years ago. Had to back when I worked for my father."

Now that she was allowing herself a really good look, Elle acknowledged that Cam and Jasper barely resembled each other. Jasper was all light hair and crystal-blue eyes, tall but lanky, while Cam was dark and large. Both brothers were attractive—beyond attractive, really—but in very different ways.

"Do you even have a key to get in?" Cam's question burst her bubble and she finally exited the truck.

"No worries." After she walked to the small front porch, she bent over and smiled as her fingers touched the key in its usual place under the decorative ceramic frog that held watch at the front door.

Cam dragged her bags into the house and stepped back onto the porch. She turned to thank him for the ride, but before she could get the words out, he put his hand on the top of the door frame. Even though she could—and should—take a step backward into the open living room, she didn't move. His eyes raked over her entire body until she squirmed.

"I'm glad you're back, Elle." Then he abruptly turned and walked back to his waiting truck.

With that, she nodded, wondering why she suddenly felt light-headed.

Cam considered himself to be a rational, sane man, but something happened to him when he saw Ellie Owens again. And that reaction defied reasoning.

"Damn," he said aloud as he drove away from her house and made his way back down Bay View Road. When he reached the fork, he started veering toward town before he remembered that he'd left his favorite cordless drill at his parents' house the night before.

Yanking the steering wheel to the left just in time, he made his way toward the east side of the bay. He'd been called by his mother to fix a shelf. Funny how when he'd arrived, tools in tow, there was nothing to fix. Instead— surprise, surprise—an attractive woman had been seated in one of the living rooms. His mother's interior designer this time.

Cam loved his mom, but her attempts at fixing him up had been increasing at a fast pace over the last two years— ever since he'd turned thirty. Even if he'd been onboard with her efforts, she clearly didn't know his tastes. Cam preferred a certain kind of woman. When his thoughts turned back to Elle, he swerved again before righting the truck.

Little Ellie Owens, who used to keep her head in a book, or in a sketch pad, while wearing jeans with patches over the knees. She'd never stepped a toe out of line until that idiotic video surfaced. Cam remembered how embarrassed Jasper had been seeing her announce her undying love for him. In Cam's opinion, it never seemed like much of a burden to have a woman show you some love. Especially a woman as grounded as Elle. Of course, Jasper had been in a pretty serious relationship back then.

Regardless, somewhere along the line, she'd grown up into a gorgeous, stunning woman. Gone was the plain-Jane scholar. In her place was an accomplished, interesting person.

Cam turned into the gates of the mansion at 1954 Bay View Road and offered a wave to Stan, the head gardener. Then he parked his truck, and ran in the back door to retrieve his drill. He was about to climb back into the truck when he noticed that not only were his parents' cars in the driveway, but so was his brother's. Cam climbed the steps to the front porch and pushed his way inside the large and impressive house he'd been lucky enough to grow up in.

He heard the shouting before he even entered the solarium.

"It's not that big of a deal."

"You think you can come in here and start making changes like you own the place?" his father asked.

"I kind of do own the place."

"Not yet," his mother's voice rang out. "Not while your father and I are still in charge."

Cam didn't have to be in the room to know that Jasper would be rolling his eyes the same way he was doing himself at the usual argument. His parents and brother butted heads on a daily basis.

"If you'd only let me implement a few small changes. Tweaks," he added quickly. "We need a better social media plan. Our communications department is currently living in the stone age figuring out how to make fire."

"It's like you don't even want to be part of this company, the way you keep trying to change everything." Cam could hear the frustration in his father's voice.

His own stomach clenched at the comment.

"Of course I want to be part of the company. Why else

would I be here?" Jasper replied. "I'm simply trying to bring us into this century."

Feeling a thickness in his throat, Cam decided to save his baby brother. Giving a quick cough to announce his presence, he stepped into the room.

"There's my handsome son." Lilah Dumont rose and patted him on the cheek before pulling him into a hug.

"Hey," Jasper called out. "I thought I was your handsome son."

She turned back to him. "Oh, you are. But only when you aren't irritating me with new proposals involving hashtags."

Cam hoped that Jasper saw the look of adoring, unaffected love their mother shot in his direction. But by the way Jasper had turned toward the window, he suspected not.

"Hey, Pops," Cam said to his dad.

"Why aren't you at work?" his dad asked as a reply and a welcome.

"Why aren't any of you?" he countered.

"We are working." His mother poured a glass of lemonade and handed it to him. "We're discussing your brother's latest idea." She used air quotes and Cam was fairly certain he could hear Jasper grind his teeth. "Then we were going to talk about the next fund-raiser."

Cam lifted an eyebrow. "Fund-raiser?"

"Yes."

"Ah. A party," he stated. His mother could justify giving a party more easily than some people could drink a glass of water. Although Lilah Dumont was so much more than a party-loving socialite. She could make just as many deals as his father simply by schmoozing during a black-tie event. Where Collin Dumont was old-school business etiquette, Lilah was about face-to-face interaction. Underestimating either her intelligence or business savvy had been the web that caught more than one misjudging fly.

"Social media is an inexpensive way to throw a party," Jasper contributed from the corner. "A virtual party. Keeps costs in check, connects you with the right people."

"Why not be personal? Why does everything have to be over the computer or smartphone or Instagram?" his mother asked. "People like personal interactions. That still means something."

Cam thought he would try and back his brother up. "Jasper does have a point. Perhaps we need to cut down on the amount of parties?"

His mother looked indignant. "Everyone loves our parties. You know that."

"Isn't less more in this situation?"

Lilah rolled her eyes. "Less is never more. I despise that saying."

On this one topic, his mother and father were in agreement. Cam had to suppress a groan. If another Dumont party was on the horizon, that meant he would have to take out his tux—again—and put on a happy face—again. Two things he hated almost as much as his mother's parties.

Jasper appeared to have forgotten his earlier hurt and turned to Cam. "Why aren't you working your butt off somewhere? Aren't you usually covered in dirt and sweat by this hour?"

"I had a meeting with a client earlier this morning." He grabbed an apple from a large display of fruit placed in the middle of a marble table. "You'll never guess who I picked up after that."

"It's bad enough that you drive that thing instead of a real car," Jasper began.

"Hey, I like my truck. I'd like you to know that Lamborghinis are not the only car available. Anyway, I did a favor for Ted Owens this morning."

"His doctor's appointment," his dad said from his chair. "I need to give him a call later and see how that went."

There were a lot of things that could be said about Collin Dumont, but one area Cam thought his dad did right. He respected his staff, his friends and the other citizens of Bayside. He'd been friends with Ted for years, and Cam heard the note of concern in his voice.

"Right. He had an appointment, so I had to pick up his daughter."

"Ellie?" his mother asked. "She's back from Italy?"

"Who's Ellie?" Jasper wondered.

Sometimes Cam didn't know if he should be appalled by or jealous of his brother's ignorance.

"You've gotta be kidding me, right?" Cam said. "Ellie Owens, the daughter of Ted, former chief of police." At Jasper's blank stare, he continued. "You were in the same class in school."

"Did we date?"

Their mother let out a loud chuckle. "Oh, most certainly not."

"She was in love with you," Cam said loudly and slowly, to get through to Jasper.

"Didn't she make some video about you that got played at your prom?" their father asked from behind the iPad he was now reading.

Cam tensed. He'd never understood why Elle had made that video in the first place. The whole thing was out of character. Feeling oddly protective, Cam decided to steer the conversation away from the video talk. "She's back. I'm not sure for how long, but she's here now for her dad. She looks amazing, by the way. All grown up."

"No kidding?" Jasper's tune changed quicker than he could get his Lamborghini from zero to sixty.

"Apparently Europe agreed with her."

"Good for her," Mrs. Dumont put in as she poured more

lemonade into her glass. "I always thought she was sweet. And everyone knew how smart she was. Top of her and Jasper's class. Or she would have been…"

"Didn't she throw herself in the bay after that prom?" Collin asked.

Another aspect of that story that had never made sense to Cam. Supposedly, she'd been so upset after the video aired that she'd pitched herself off the dock into the bay. Some called it a last-ditch effort to get Jasper's attention.

"Oh, yeah," Jasper replied.

The thing about attempting to drown yourself was that people who did so usually couldn't swim, Cam thought. Elle had been a great swimmer. He shook his head. A mystery for another time.

"Invite her to the party on Friday," Collin contributed, still reading his iPad, no doubt having pulled up the *Wall Street Journal*.

"Great idea," Lilah added.

"Um, I don't know if that's…"

"I'm willing to extend the olive branch to a hot girl," Jasper said.

Cam ignored his brother's wink. "Did you say Friday? The party is happening this Friday? It's Wednesday."

"Invitations went out two days ago. What is life without a little surprise and excitement?" His mother's eyes sparkled.

"I didn't get an invitation," Cam said.

"That's because I didn't want to give you a chance to RSVP no." Lilah beamed at him.

Cam clenched his teeth. He'd had plans to quit work early on Friday and take a couple of his employees golfing. "What's the reason for this party?" he asked.

They all looked at each other for a split second before his mother said "April," with a definite nod.

At the same moment his father said, "Flag Day."

Cam rolled his eyes, not sure where to start.

"Oh, who cares why," his mother called out. "It's a party, not a funeral, so get that stick out of your a—"

"Ah, that's enough," Collin said, as Cam tucked his tongue in the side of this mouth.

"But you are expected to be there," Lilah said, using her I-raised-two-boys-so-don't-even-think-about-messing-with-me tone.

"Seriously, Mom." Cam put his glass down on the table a little harder than he'd meant to and returned the uneaten apple, as well. The sound of heavy crystal hitting marble echoed throughout the room. For a moment, no one spoke. Then Collin looked up from his iPad.

"Just because you didn't want to work for the family doesn't mean you're not part of it."

Cam hated the hurt that flashed in his father's eyes. He knew he'd put it there by one selfish decision. He began to speak to his dad, but Jasper stopped him.

"Don't be so hard on him. I stepped up. I work for the family."

Cam knew Jasper wasn't saying that out of spite. He was only trying to help.

"And what an employee you turned out to be. Always wanting to change every damn little thing."

That same painful look flashed in Jasper's eyes now and Cam wanted to kick himself. He hadn't planned to come in here today to upset everyone. Nor had he intended to cause so much ill will when he stopped working for his parents and started his own company.

But it didn't take a soured afternoon to see the results of his decision. He carried around the guilt on a daily basis.

Cam used to go to every construction site of every building, shopping mall, apartment complex or whatever else his dad had been working on. Collin had proudly introduced him as the future head of Dumont Industries to anyone who would listen. That included Rick, the foreman on one of his job sites.

Rick had been the first person to really talk to Cam about construction. He'd patiently answered question after question. Walking around wearing a hard hat, looking at foundations and I beams made Cam feel excited. Not once had he ever felt that way in the office with his dad.

One summer Cam had announced that he would be working with Rick on the construction of a new multiplex. His dad still hadn't realized that Cam liked working with his hands, enjoyed building things. Instead, Collin had bragged that his son wanted to learn the business from the ground up, and wasn't that just great.

But even as a sixteen-year-old, Cam knew he'd found his calling. His dad never forgave him for it.

Cam pulled himself back to the present when his father let out an awkward and forced cough.

"I need to take this." He waved his phone and made a quick exit from the room, hurt trailing in his wake.

Cam didn't look at his mother when she rose from her seat, nor did he say goodbye as he left the solarium and headed back through the sprawling house toward the front door. He turned only when he heard his brother's voice.

"Cam, wait." Jasper bounded toward him, his expression concerned.

"Don't worry about it," Cam said. "And don't listen to the old man. You're doing a great job."

Jasper's face fell. "Yeah, I can't get my own father to listen to my ideas, let alone the rest of the board. Quick, someone get me on the cover of *Forbes*."

Cam didn't know what to say and he couldn't stand seeing the frustration in his brother's eyes. "Listen, I'll stop by your place later and fix that balcony door."

Jasper shook his head.

"What?" Cam asked. "It's been hanging off the hinges

for weeks. And while I'm there I can measure for those shelves you were talking about."

"Stop," Jasper said. "You don't owe me anything, Cam."

But he did. Cam was in debt to his little brother and fixing a few things around his condo didn't even come close to making up for it.

"I'll be by around seven," he said, his voice offering no room for argument. With his hand on the brass doorknob of the opulent front door, he asked his baby brother, "Are you happy?"

"What?"

"Answer the damn question, Jasp."

Jasper let out a long exhalation. "I'm fine. Stop worrying about me. Things are going fine."

But he did worry about him. More than his brother realized. Because Jasper had stepped up for him and Cam would spend the rest of his life making it right.

"Hey, bro. Answer me this." Cam waited for Jasper to meet his eyes. "Do you really not remember Elle Owens?"

Jasper shrugged. "Kind of. But if you say she's gorgeous now…"

Unbelievable. Because to Cam's way of thinking, the woman he'd picked up this morning was pretty damn unforgettable.

"I never said *gorgeous*." But he very easily could have. Suddenly, Cam felt incredibly uncomfortable.

His brother grinned as Cam flipped him off and left the house, thoughts of just how gorgeous Elle had become following him out the door.

Chapter Two

"Cancer free as of today."

The breath she let out was full of relief. Elle had been holding her jaw so tight that her face actually ached.

"Seriously?" she asked tentatively. She knew better than anyone that her dad had a habit of downplaying. The fact that he hadn't shared his diagnosis—even during their recent Christmas visit—until a couple weeks ago still had her seeing red.

"Cross my heart." Her dad kissed her on the head before engulfing her in a long, hard hug. Nothing could have felt better. "I'm sorry I wasn't there to pick you up this morning."

"Oh, don't worry about that." She waved a hand in the air as she took in her father. He looked mostly the same, a little thinner maybe, and a bit pale. But that was to be expected. "Tell me everything the doctor said, and start from the beginning."

Even though he rolled his eyes, Elle held firm. She would get the truth of the situation even if that meant calling the doctor herself.

"Our food is going to get cold," he said, gesturing to the spread on the table.

"It won't if you hurry up and tell me."

"You've always been the most stubborn little thing," he said with a laugh.

She returned with a chuckle of her own. "Wonder where I get that trait from."

"Fine, fine. The treatment seemed to work. When I went back in today, doc said the scope we did last week didn't detect any cancerous cells."

He was beaming and Elle wanted to share in his joy, but she'd done a fair amount of research on bladder cancer. They would need to stay on top of this to ensure it didn't return. Her dad would have to get scopes often and probably for the rest of his life.

A small concession for keeping him in her life. With her mother already passed, Elle would do anything to protect her only remaining parent. Even though she barely remembered her mom, she wanted to think that her returning from Italy would have made her proud.

But for the moment, she'd try and enjoy the victory with him. She reached for a pair of wineglasses when an invitation on the counter caught her eye.

Her father followed her gaze. "Mrs. Dumont is having another party on Friday and the theme is *Printemps*." He rolled his eyes as he took the wineglasses from her hands.

"Springtime," Elle murmured. "Well, that's a fitting theme." She leaned back against the counter. "Are you going to attend?"

He let out a loud chuckle. "That'll be the day. Don't know why they even invite me to those damn dreaded things."

Elle smiled and they sat down at the table and toasted with a bottle of wine she'd brought back from Italy.

"To your health," she announced, her glass held in the air.

"To my baby girl being home."

"Cin cin." With that, they clinked glasses.

To celebrate her return, they were enjoying a huge bowl of spaghetti and meatballs. Her father had insisted on cooking "his specialty." Elle had to laugh. She couldn't even begin to count the number of times they'd feasted on this exact meal when she'd been growing up.

Not to mention that she'd lived in Italy for the last six years, plus one year of study abroad in college. She'd been spoiled by the outstanding culinary pleasures of Italy. But watching her father slurp up his spaghetti, with sauce dotting his chin, seeing the pride when he announced that he'd heated up the frozen meatballs and garlic bread, made this the best pasta she'd ever tasted.

As they ate, Elle filled her dad in on her flight and he told her some of the local Bayside gossip. A nice breeze came off the bay and filled the house with the awakening scents of early spring.

"I have a friend in Florence who would go nuts over this," Elle said, referring to the chocolate éclair her father had bought at the local bakery.

"Speaking of people you know in Italy…"

Oh, jeez. Her dad was anything but subtle.

"What about that nice fellow I met at Christmas when I was visiting?" he asked.

"Marco," she said.

"Yeah, him. He seemed nice."

Marco was great. Sexy and sweet. They'd dated for the last year. "I didn't know how long I would be here and neither of us wanted a long-distance relationship."

"You don't have to have one. Why did you come back to Bayside, Ellie?"

His question stung. Did he not want his only child here with him? *For you. Because I was worried about you, of course.* "I guess I just needed a change of scenery."

"You guess, huh? Well, I just hope somebody wasn't worried that their aging dad needed a chaperone…"

Biting back a smile, she shook her head. "Never."

"Ellie…"

"Elle, Dad. I go by Elle now."

"Right, sorry." He patted her cheek. "You know you'll always be my little Ellie." The uncharacteristic sentimentality came and went before she could blink. Quickly, her dad returned to his usual pragmatic ex-cop self. "I'm worried. What are you going to do here? There aren't any galleries or museums in the area."

She chewed on her lip before rising to close the window. The truth was she had no idea what she would do for work. She'd contacted every museum within an hour's drive of Bayside—not many—and come up empty-handed. Italy might have the most fantastic jobs for her, but Bayside had her family. A family that she had been desperately worried about.

Financially, she would be okay for a couple months, especially with her father refusing her offer of paying rent. Still, she'd need to find some kind of job.

Returning to her seat, she looked at her father. "I'm working on it. Don't worry."

He pinned her with one of his cop stares. "'Don't worry.' When you have a kid someday you'll realize how stupid that little statement is."

Elle followed her dad when he rose from the table, taking their plates into the kitchen. "Daddy…"

Dropping a plate, he spun back to face her. "I will always worry about you."

Sighing, she did the only thing she could think of. She wrapped her arms around her dad until he relented and returned the embrace. "I know you will, and that's why I love you."

Finally, he let out a deep sigh. "I guess that will have to be enough for now."

They finished clearing and cleaning the dishes. Then her dad did something she'd greatly missed while she'd been away. He turned on the radio to an oldies station, the music wafted throughout the house. Happily, she sat down with him in the living room as he perused the daily paper and she pretended to do the crossword puzzle.

"So, Cam Dumont picked me up today." She surprised herself with the comment, unsure what made Cam spring into her mind. But now that she was thinking about him, there wasn't any harm in remembering the way his worn jeans had fit him so perfectly. Or how the masculine, dark stubble on his face had produced butterflies in her stomach. How would it feel against her cheeks?

"Cam's a good guy."

"Yeah, he seemed…great." She eyed her dad who wasn't taking her bait for more info.

"What are your plans for tomorrow?"

Elle sat back considering. She had no idea. With no job and no friends, she didn't have many options.

As if reading her mind, her dad said, "Why don't you go check out The Brewside? It's a coffee shop that opened about two years ago," he explained. "It's right in the town square."

"I could do that. Maybe I could bring my sketch pad, too."

Before she'd moved over to the administrative side of the art world, she'd dreamed of becoming an artist in her own right. Then she'd become so immersed in her career, not to mention all the other amazing opportunities afforded her living in Italy, that her favorite hobby had been pushed to the back burner.

Energized by the idea of taking time for her own art, she grinned.

"You look more and more beautiful every time I see you." The compliment, not to mention the change in conversation, took her by surprise, but the soft tone of her dad's voice almost undid her.

"Oh, Daddy. You saw me three months ago. I haven't changed since then."

He picked up a silver-framed picture from the end table. Without seeing it, Elle knew it was a shot of her at fifteen, after she'd climbed a tree. She was wearing cutoff jeans and an unfortunate maroon sweatshirt, her hair in pigtails displaying her makeup-free face, which had been going through an adolescent breakout phase. She'd been so clueless.

Her dad turned the photo around. "You've changed a lot since this. The time goes so fast," he said, more to himself than to her.

"I think it's time for you to go to bed. A weepy daddy is a tired daddy."

"You might be right about that. It's been a long day, but a good one. Welcome home, princess." He kissed her forehead and made his way toward his bedroom.

Feeling antsy, Elle put down the crossword puzzle, grabbed an afghan from the couch and made her way out onto the deck. The water was calm tonight, and as usual for this time of year, the temperature was dropping rapidly. She wrapped the blanket around herself as the sounds of the water lapping soothed her.

Looking up, she gazed at the sky, full of glittery stars. It was strange to think that last night she'd seen the same stars from across the ocean. Now she was back in her hometown, not quite sure how that fact made her feel.

For the second time that night, Cam entered her mind. She wasn't sure how she felt about that either.

Why in the world was she thinking about a man she hadn't seen in a decade and spent a whopping thirty minutes with? It didn't make sense. And yet, she couldn't seem to stop.

She shook her head. Most likely, she was overly tired from a long day of travel and an emotional reunion with her father. That had to be the only reason she couldn't stop thinking about Cam's enticing smile, his mysterious eyes, his amazing body.

Obviously, being with her dad was her number one priority. Just eating dinner with him and seeing with her own two eyes that he was okay made her feel better. But her dad and this tiny house were only a small part of Bayside. Tomorrow she had to face the rest of the town.

Elle knew she'd come a long way since that picture her father had looked at earlier. Undoubtedly, she'd changed. Now she just had to figure out to how convince everyone else.

After seeing her dad off to work the next morning, Elle set off to check out The Brewside, sketch pad in tow.

As she walked along the path next to the bay, the cool morning air hit her face. It felt great after a restless night's sleep. She'd finally fallen to sleep in the wee hours only to wake up around four thirty. Stupid jet lag.

And perhaps Cam Dumont kept her tossing and turning, too.

But she was not going to dwell on that little detail. Even if she was wondering where he lived. And where he'd set up his business. And what he did for fun.

She stopped in her tracks. "Stop thinking about Cameron Dumont," she whispered. With a nod, she continued on her way.

She found The Brewside Café easily enough. Nestled between a shoe store that had been in the square forever and a newer, expensive-looking clothing shop, it was painted the same crisp white, accented with blue shutters, as the other establishments. Pots of flowers flanked the entrance. She pushed open the door to the sound of bells chiming and was hit with the welcoming aroma of rich coffee beans.

Inhaling, Elle stood there for a moment, soaking in the

caffeine goodness. Once she had her fill, she stepped inside and took in the quaint decor. The raised ceiling was supported by exposed beams, and the dark wood floors gave the place a rustic feel. The tables were made up of wooden barrels with either glass plates or old doors on top. Copper pots and old kitchen utensils adorned the walls, as did a variety of vinyl records and framed black-and-white photographs. A display case with pastries dominated one wall and a large bar with coffee machines and an antique brass cash register stretched along the back.

After studying the menu, Elle stepped forward and ordered an espresso and a wheat bagel. As one of the workers began filling her order, a tall man with a beard and friendly blue eyes stopped wiping the counter and studied her.

"Hi, I'm Tony. I own this place," he finally said.

Elle shook his hand. "Oh, nice to meet you. I'm—"

"Ellie Owens. I know."

"How do you know?" She couldn't place him and was pretty sure they hadn't gone to high school together.

"Offering a legal, addictive stimulant every morning makes me the best friend of pretty much everyone in town. I have a knack for remembering faces and I've never seen yours before." He picked up a copy of the local paper and handed it to her. "Plus, you've been outed."

"Excuse me?"

"By the Bayside Blogger. You made both the online and print versions of the paper."

She stared at the front page of the newspaper. "Who's the Bayside Blogger?"

"Only the most popular columnist in the whole *Bayside Bugle*." A woman wearing a flurry of bright colors planted herself by Elle's side. "Riley Hudson," she announced. "We graduated in the same class."

Right. Riley Hudson of the Hudson family that had lived in Bayside for so many generations many people thought they'd probably discovered it. If Elle remembered correctly, Riley had been the most outgoing person in their class, popular, pretty and always dressed like she'd just stepped out of a fashion magazine. Basically, she'd been Elle's polar opposite in high school. Given how she looked now, her fashion sense hadn't changed. She was wearing a chartreuse A-line dress, a cute little fuchsia scarf and matching sunglasses perched atop a head of thick, wavy red hair.

"Hi, Riley. Nice to see you again."

"You, too. Welcome back."

While Riley said hello to Tony and put in an order for a nonfat latte, Elle quickly scanned the paper. The headline Lovesick Ellie Owens Returns to Bayside, splashed across the front page of section C, almost made her choke on her drink. The article following went on to sum up her brief, yet crazy history with Jasper, with an even quicker mention of her time in Italy.

Did people really read this? Did her dad? Biting her lip, Elle pushed down an uneasy feeling. She'd embarrassed her father beyond belief back in high school, and the last thing she wanted to do was repeat the past.

Elle turned her attention back to Riley as the other woman said, "If you want to know anything about the Bayside Blogger, just ask me. I read her column religiously. It's like the *New York Post*'s Page Six, only here in Bayside. Want to sit together?"

Elle found her energy infectious. She nodded and followed Riley to a table. "So it's like a gossip column?"

"It's annoying." This came from the guy behind the counter who had filled Elle's order. "Damn Blogger got me in trouble with my girlfriend when she reported that I had been out with my buddies at the Beer Bash."

"You were at the Beer Bash, Brody. I saw you," Riley stated.

"But maybe I told Elizabeth that I would be watching a game over at Alan's that night."

Riley rolled her big emerald green eyes. "That's your fault then. The Blogger was simply reporting the truth."

He moved away, mumbling something under his breath that sounded a lot like "damn busybody." Riley smiled and turned her attention back to Elle. "Are you excited to be back?"

"I guess." She couldn't hold in a long yawn. "Sorry. I'm jet-lagged."

"Living in Europe for six years. That's so glamorous. What did you do there?" Riley added a couple packets of sweetener to her latte and then sat back with a moony look on her face. "I imagine you lounging at cafés for hours with hot Italian men hanging on to your every word. I see plates of sinful pasta and caprese salads and you drinking amazing wine while tourists rush into the Duomo behind you."

Elle laughed at the imagery. "The wine part's true enough." She leaned across the table and lowered her voice. "But you forgot about the shoes. Oh, the amazing designer shoes."

An appreciative sigh escaped Riley's lips. "You're killing me. Hashtag, jealous."

After sampling her bagel, Elle took another sip of coffee. "I wish I could tell you it was all play and no work, but truthfully, I did have to make a living. Even in a country as laid-back as Italy, they tend to expect payment for things like housing and food."

"Sticklers." Riley shook her head. "What did you do?"

"My last job was at an up-and-coming gallery right around the corner from the Duomo. But I've worked in a ton of museums there."

Riley looked down. Noticing Elle's sketch pad, she pointed at it. "Are you an artist, Ellie Owens?"

There was a certain awe in the question that filled her with pride. "It's a hobby, and actually, I go by Elle now."

"No more Ellie?" Riley cocked her head.

"Let's just say I retired her a long time ago. So, what do you do now?"

Riley ran a hand along her plaid computer bag. "I'm a writer."

Elle smiled. "That would explain the colorful descriptions. What do you write?"

"I'd like to write the next great American novel. Or at least a really juicy romance novel devoured by women at every beach in the country. But for the moment I'm a reporter with the *Bayside Bugle*. I write for the Style & Entertainment section."

Something from earlier niggled at her brain. "Wait a minute." Elle put her bagel down. "If you write for the *Bugle*, you must know who this Bayside Blogger is."

"I wish. I have friends that have offered me big money to reveal her identity. Sadly, the only person who knows is our editor in chief, Sawyer. He's also received offers of money, concert tickets, home-cooked meals, you name it. But he won't budge."

"Sawyer Wallace? Wasn't he a couple years older than us in school?"

"Two," Riley confirmed.

"Didn't he drill a hole between the boys' and girls' locker rooms once so he could get an eyeful?"

Tony chuckled from behind the bar.

"Annoying then and annoying now. He hasn't changed."

But Riley's face did. Elle couldn't help but notice her cheeks redden. Interesting. As interesting as the fact that she'd just spoken more to Riley Hudson in the last ten minutes than all of high school. Not that Riley had ever been mean to her. But they'd run in very different circles.

The bells above the door jingled and in walked none

other than Cam Dumont. Elle looked up as Riley waved a hot-pink nail-polished hand and called, "Hey, good-looking."

"If it isn't the girl trying to turn Bayside into her own version of sophisticated Manhattan," he replied.

"One small step at a time. Speaking of elegance and style, I got the invite to your mother's *Printemps* soiree. You know I'll be there."

"You and the rest of the planet." Cam rolled his eyes and turned toward Elle. "Morning, Elle."

"Hi, Cam. Nice to see you again."

He moved to the counter and placed an order for an extra-large coffee to go. While he talked with Tony, Elle couldn't help but notice once again the way Cam's worn jeans clung to certain places in a really awesome way. In fact, now that she was observing, she had to admit that with his tall, muscular body, slight stubble on his chiseled face and too-long dark hair, Cam Dumont was a nice healthy dose of man candy. No wonder she kept thinking about him last night. And this morning.

She could only imagine that when he got to work and slung a tool belt around his waist he would become even more appealing. And maybe if it was a hot day and he needed to take off his shirt...

"So, Elle, have you seen Jasper yet?"

Elle sloshed the remainder of her espresso onto the newspaper. She accepted the napkins Riley offered, even as she became aware that Cam, Tony, Brody and the table of older men sitting on the other side of the room all turned in her direction at the question. She felt she should have some grand, detailed story to tell Riley in answer, when really the truth was simple. "Nope," she said softly.

"Well, you'll definitely see him at the *Printemps* party tomorrow night."

"Actually, I'm not going to the party," Elle said.

Riley appeared taken aback, as if Elle had just reached across the table and slapped her. "Excuse me? Hold the presses. Why in the world are you not coming tomorrow?" Her hands gestured wildly and her mouth went into a pout.

Elle laughed. "For one thing, I wasn't invited."

"But your dad probably was. Oh, by the way, I'm so sorry to hear about his cancer. How's he doing? You have to come tomorrow," she continued, without taking a breath. "I'll introduce you to the new faces of Bayside. Not that there's many."

Blame it on the jet lag, but Elle didn't know if she could keep up with Riley.

"Oh, my God, there's this guy I should totally set you up with. I mean, unless you're still stuck on Jasper."

Cam cleared his throat, calling both women's attention to him. "Uh, yeah. I'm supposed to invite you to the party tomorrow." He didn't meet her eyes. Instead, he looked into his cup of coffee as if it held all the answers of the universe.

Jeez, Elle thought. Could he be less excited? He made it sound like he was inviting her to a mass murder.

"Aww, Cam, are you inviting Elle? That's sweet."

"I'm not. My mom wanted me to."

Even better. And why did it bother her that he wasn't the one inviting her to the party? "I probably shouldn't go," she began.

Eyes shining, Cam let out a huge breath. Then he took a long swig of coffee. "Yeah, probably better."

Hold on, did Cam not want her to go? Why the hell not? Because of the video?

Buoyed by a sudden stubbornness, she said, "You know, on second thought, maybe I *should* stop by. I mean, since your mom extended the invitation to me and all."

Riley clapped her hands together in quick succession. "Yeah."

Cam's face fell. "Are you sure? It's, ah, a formal, black-tie kind of party."

"Not a problem. I recently bought a gown when I was visiting Milan. It'll be just perfect for the occasion."

Did he think she couldn't afford a gown or something? That she'd never been to a formal party? She may not have a bank account like his but, hell, who did? Besides, Elle couldn't figure out why he wouldn't want her there. But she'd show him. Not only would she go to that party, but she'd look better than she ever had in her entire life.

"A gown from Milan? Oh, my God, you are like the coolest person I know. I must raid your closet immediately."

Elle smiled at Riley even as she watched Cam seething.

"My mother's parties are overrated. Trust me," he said through clenched teeth.

Enough was enough. She was tired, a little overwhelmed and greatly annoyed. She stood and turned to Cam. Trying to get up in his face proved difficult, considering her five feet six inches didn't come close to his height. Still, she tilted her chin up and pegged him with her most intimidating stare.

"Maybe I should come to that conclusion myself."

Riley stayed silent as she watched the two of them from the table with an interested look on her face.

"It's not going to go the way you want," Cam said quietly, so only she could hear.

"What way is that, exactly?"

He looked as if he wanted to say something. His mouth even opened slightly, but no words came out. Elle could practically see the wheels churning in his brain.

"Jasper," he whispered, his eyes glued to hers.

Just as she'd suspected. Even Cam thought she would still make a fool out of herself over his brother.

It hadn't even been a full twenty-four hours since she'd

returned and she already felt like a total outcast. Stupidly, she'd thought a full decade away would have given everyone ample time to forget about that one little moment when she'd lost her mind.

Her cheeks felt warm as she tried to hold the embarrassment at bay. She wanted to yell at Cam, tell him she wasn't some girl obsessed with her high school crush. Truthfully, she didn't know how she'd feel seeing Jasper again. Her stomach tightened at the thought of it. But she was back in Bayside, so she knew it would happen eventually. What did Cam think? She would see his brother and throw herself at his feet?

How many other people would assume the same?

Beyond frustrated with Cam and his presumptions, she gathered her things and nodded to Riley. Then she narrowed her eyes at Cam. "I wouldn't miss this party for anything in the world, Cameron Dumont."

With that, she pushed open the door with all the dignity she could muster.

Chapter Three

"Elle, wait up!" Cam called as he rushed out of The Brewside. It had taken him one whole second to realize he'd really hurt her feelings.

It wasn't that he didn't want Elle to come tomorrow night. It was more that he didn't want her to become upset at the party when the local gossips would no doubt descend on her like a scene from Hitchcock's *The Birds*.

And dammit, he knew she'd changed. Jasper had changed, too. But the rest of Bayside? Still the same. *That* was the problem.

Bayside was his home and he loved it. But that didn't mean he was oblivious to the inherent small-town quirks—like gossip, clinging to the past and more gossip.

Elle and Jasper in the same room with the entire town watching was a recipe for disaster.

But at the moment, Cam needed to find Elle and explain. Or at the very least, apologize. He spotted her light brown hair blowing in the soft breeze coming off the water. She was halfway across the square. He rushed in that direction.

"Elle, hang on."

"I'm done talking to you." She kept walking.

Finally close enough to stop her, Cam reached for her arm. He grabbed hold for a second before she shook him off and turned around to face him. "What is your problem?"

"I only wanted to say…"

"What?" she snapped.

"I'm sorry."

"Well—oh."

By the way she blinked multiple times in rapid succession without any words coming out of her mouth, he'd obviously taken her by surprise. She started biting her lip, and then squinted up at him.

"I think you got the wrong impression back there," he said. "My parents' parties…" He threw his hands up in the air. "They are… I mean, it's just that the people that go… I really don't…"

Her face fell and she shrugged. "I get it. You don't want me there. You think I'll make a scene and ruin the event. Is that what you're trying to say?"

"No."

"Then *what*?" she asked.

"I hate those parties."

There, he'd said it out loud. He'd never really told anyone that before, although he was sure many people assumed as much. After all, a surly guy hanging out in the corner, downing beer instead of expensive, imported champagne, and talking to as few people as possible, might give off the impression he wasn't the party-loving animal the rest of the Dumonts were. He felt almost guilty admitting that. Like he was betraying his family, and hadn't he already done that when he'd shirked his birthright and started his own company?

"You hate the parties? Really?" She emitted a little laugh.

"Why are you laughing?"

"It's funny. Unless they've drastically changed, your parents' parties are supposed to rival…" she tapped a finger against her lips, pausing in thought "…Oscar parties, inaugural balls, royal weddings."

His turn to laugh. "Can't say I know about any of those things. Listen, I don't think you'd make a scene tomorrow, although to be honest, it would be a hell of a lot more fun if you did."

"Cam." She rolled her eyes, but was smiling as she did so.

She had a nice smile. Really nice, he noticed. It brightened up her face and brought out those adorable dimples in her cheeks.

And the sun was catching her hair, casting a golden hue on the brown tresses.

"Cam," she repeated. "Tell me the real reason you don't want me to come to the party."

He looked around the square, at the stores that hadn't yet opened for the day. Some wouldn't open at all, their owners here only for the busy summer tourist season. In the distance, he could hear the squawking of gulls as a fishing boat no doubt returned to the bay.

Bayside was home. It always would be. There was something comforting about that.

"You know," he said, gesturing vaguely. "Some things have changed around here since you left. But others, not so much."

Elle nodded even as she narrowed her eyes. "That's kind of the way of the world."

"One of the things that changed… I mean, you really should know something." He wasn't doing this right.

"What is it?"

He studied her face for a long moment before running a hand through his hair. "Nothing. Never mind."

"You sure?"

He decided to avoid her question and change the subject instead. "So, do you really have some fancy dress from Milan?"

Elle smiled. "I don't know about fancy. I was going more for sophisticated. But yes, I have a dress from Milan."

"Did you go there often?"

She bit her lip, considering. "I went every so often. What I really loved was taking weekend trips to Southern Italy. Naples has the best food."

Cam found himself genuinely interested. How could he not be when she became so animated talking about a country that she clearly loved. Her eyes were practically sparkling.

"I thought all of the food in Italy was amazing," he offered.

She licked her lips, an enticing gesture that drew his gaze right to her.

"Oh, it is. Trust me. There's no salt in the food in Tuscany, which takes some getting used to. But once you do..." She kissed her fingers. *"Molto bene. Delizioso."*

There was something really appealing about this woman. It went beyond her looks, which were obviously stunning. But something else drew him to her.

"Of course, the wine is insane. Chianti was a personal favorite. And don't even get me started on the gelato." She winked at him. "I'm really going to miss that."

"I've seen gelato here," Cam said.

Her face fell. "It won't be the same."

"Hey," he said, reaching out and touching her arm. "You sure you're okay being back here?"

She glanced around the square, a million thoughts crossing her face. She let out a long sigh.

"Elle?" he prompted.

"I will be fine. I know it. I've missed it here."

"But you're going to miss Italy, too." He said it rather

than asked it because it was so clear she was struggling with this move.

Cam rolled back on his heels as he studied her. She had really beautiful eyes. They were so expressive, yet inquisitive. He bet she didn't miss much. Including her father's recent health scare. Cam had to hand it to her. She could have come back for a short visit. Instead, she'd dropped her life, all the things she adored, to return to Bayside.

She gave up her life for her dad. It caused a pit to form in his stomach. She'd run toward her family while he'd run from his and everything they offered.

"Hey, you okay?" she asked. Cam had been right. She was perceptive.

Without overthinking it, he said, "You're pretty amazing, Elle."

Those fabulous eyes widened. "Thank you…Jasper."

Momentarily confused, Cam realized that Elle was looking over his shoulder. Turning, he saw his brother strolling from his car toward The Brewside.

Jasper turned in their direction and gave a small wave to Cam, before he took in Elle.

Could he be more obvious about giving her a long once-over?

Once he'd assessed Elle, he quickly switched courses and headed their way.

"Good morning," he called.

"Hey, Jasp, what are you doing in town? Shouldn't you be at the office already?"

Cam really didn't care about the answer to that question. He was too busy watching Elle for her reaction. She was smiling as she noted his brother approaching.

"I have an off-site meeting first. Cam, why don't you introduce me to your lovely friend." Jasper didn't so much as look toward him as he said this. Instead, he sidled up to Elle and offered her a hand.

Cam shoved his own hands in his pockets. "You already know her."

But Jasper was shaking her hand, anyway. "I'm only kidding. How could I ever forget someone as beautiful as Ellie Owens?"

Elle pulled her hand out of Jasper's grasp. "Wow, so early for such a cheesy line."

Score one for her.

Undeterred and offering Elle what Cam liked to call "Jasper's megawatt smile," his brother leaned closer and put a hand over his heart as if it was breaking. "Ouch. But you are beautiful."

Elle leaned in as well and winked at him. "But I didn't used to be. In fact, the last time you saw me I probably looked quite different. That can only mean that someone told you I'd returned."

A crease formed on Jasper's brow. "Maybe I just remember you."

"Hmm, perhaps," Elle said with a coy smile. "Although I think you've taken me in longer this morning than you did in all our years of high school."

It wasn't often a female addled Jasper's brain, and Cam was enjoying it.

"I was an idiot in high school," his brother said, stepping forward again. Taking her hand once more, he added, "Forgive me?" with another Jasper smile.

Elle tilted her head before removing her hand yet again. "It's fine."

Shifting uncomfortably, Cam eventually elbowed his brother in the ribs.

"Ow." Shaking him off, Jasper returned his attention to Elle. "How long are you back in town?"

"I'm not sure, actually." She chewed on her lip. "I just got back from Florence yesterday."

"Did you come back with your boyfriend? Husband?"

Cam snorted, unable to hold it in. Elle shot him a look.

"Actually I just broke up with the man I was seeing. I'm single now."

"I'm sorry to hear that." Jasper snapped his fingers. "We should grab dinner some night. Catch up."

Elle studied him, appearing amused at their meeting. Besides that, Cam couldn't tell what else she was thinking. Did seeing his brother remind her of her adolescent crush? Personally, he thought Jasper was laying it on a bit thick, but he'd seen plenty of women succumb when his brother wasn't being half as charming.

"Maybe. We'll see."

Score two points for Elle. A team, Cam decided, he was firmly rooting for.

Jasper seemed confused at her reluctance. "Here," he said, pulling a business card out of his jacket pocket. "Give me a call if you change your mind." His megawatt smile appeared once more. "In the meantime, you should come to a party tomorrow."

"The *Printemps* do at your parents' house?" she asked innocently.

Jasper's face lit up. "Yes. Please come as my guest."

"Actually," Elle said, "your brother already invited me."

"My brother…" Jasper turned to him and his left eyebrow arched dramatically. "Oh, really?" He darted his gaze between the two of them, waiting for some obvious sign of understanding. "So are you going…together?" He gestured from one to the other, then leaned toward Cam and whispered, "That's faster than you usually move."

Before Cam could counter that, Elle spoke up. "No, we're not," she stated quickly.

Too quickly, Cam thought. And why should that bug him?

Jasper took a step closer. "Good to hear." He offered Elle a wink.

"Well, I really should be going. I wanted to get some sketching in today and the light is just right at the moment. But I'll see both of you tomorrow."

She began to walk away, a feminine sway to her hips that Cam knew both his and his brother's gazes were drawn to.

"Ellie Owens?" Jasper said out loud, after running a hand over his mouth.

"She goes by Elle now," Cam said, still watching her walk off.

"Little Ellie Owens?" The surprise in Jasper's voice was comical.

"The one and only," Cam said drily, slapping a hand on his brother's back as they watched Elle's retreating form.

Jasper scrubbed both hands over his face. "When you said she'd changed, you weren't kidding. She's gorgeous."

Yes, she is. "She's okay."

"Cam, come on. Too bad she didn't look like that in high school." Jasper wiggled an eyebrow for emphasis.

Shaking his head, Cam resisted the urge to sigh.

As he rubbed his hands together, Jasper's smile grew wide and playful. "Seems like the two of you have gotten cozy pretty fast. Definitely can't wait for tomorrow's party now."

Not for the first time in his life—hell, not for the first time today—Cam had to remind himself that he did in fact love his little brother. No matter how irritating he could be.

"Jasp." He snapped his fingers in front of Jasper's face. "What about Mindy?"

"Who?" he asked dreamily.

Cam groaned. "Mindy. Your girlfriend."

To his credit, Jasper bowed his head as his face reddened. Then his usual playful grin returned. "I'm kidding. She's out of town. And I wasn't hitting on Elle, so stop with the reproachful look."

"Could have fooled me."

"I was flirting. Flirting is not the same as full-on hitting on a woman. And why should it bother you, anyway? Thought you gave up dating after Spacy Stacy."

Cam's own grin came fast and wide. "Spacy Stacy was harmless." True, she became easily confused over minor details and anything involving numbers, sports or current events. But she'd been fun for a while.

"Harmless but hot. Some of my favorite traits." Jasper chuckled, but Cam knew he was only kidding.

His brother clapped him on the back. "I just want to see you happy."

"Who said I'm not happy?" Cam countered.

Jasper nodded in the direction Elle had taken. "I think maybe you could be even happier. You just have to let yourself accept it."

Cam rolled his eyes. "You sound like one of those stupid daily affirmations podcasts that Mom listens to."

Jasper pointed toward The Brewside. "I'm going to get some coffee. And don't knock the podcasts. Maybe you should listen to one before the party tomorrow. Maybe it will help you find your mojo with Elle."

Cam tried to reach out and slap him on the arm, but his brother was too fast. "I'm over dating," he yelled, but Jasper ignored him. Cam watched him walk away.

Their mother always promised fireworks at every party she threw. Between Jasper, Elle and the busybodies of Bayside, Cam feared there might be more than one kind of fireworks tomorrow night.

Chapter Four

There's nothing like a Dumont party! I'd never miss an opportunity to mingle with my faithful followers. Anonymously, of course.

Rumor has it that little Ellie Owens got invited by both Dumont brothers. Hmm, that's an interesting twist. Who do you think she'll dance with first? Check back tomorrow for the answer…

Elle's fantasies about attending a Dumont party had always been just that. A fantasy. Tonight, though, the fantasy had become reality and she was now standing outside the sprawling mansion on Bay View Road feeling very, very apprehensive.

Of course, her dad hadn't helped matters. He'd made it known that he was less than pleased she'd decided to go to the party. That only added to her nerves.

At least she was confident about her outfit. She loved the floor-length scarlet dress outlined with a thin layer of sparkly silver beading. The minute she'd seen it in the window of the boutique in Milan she'd known it was special. The dress came up around her neck but left her shoulders bare. Her figure was on full display as the sinfully silky material clung to her curves, and the slit in the skirt came up high, showing off her toned legs and the glittery heels she wore. Because of the high neckline she'd scooped her hair up into an intricate style that had taken way too much time and way too many bobby pins to secure. But with her dangly silver earrings and bright red lips, she knew the look was complete.

Drawing on that assurance, she entered the Dumont estate. She smiled at the waitstaff flanking the entrance with trays of champagne. Deciding a little liquid courage might be just the thing to calm her, she happily took a glass before giving her wrap to yet another staff member.

Since she'd never been inside the Dumont house, she took a moment to look around. Elegant staircases on either side of the foyer led up to a balcony, accented by a large crystal chandelier. As she walked across the marble floor, her heels made a *click clack* sound that echoed off walls adorned with priceless paintings. She'd like more time to get a better look at them.

Stopping at a large mirror set in an ornate gold frame, she checked her makeup and hair one last time. Satisfied, Elle took a large gulp of champagne, put the glass down and proceeded along the hallway to a set of glass doors that were immediately opened by gloved servants.

It was like an old black-and-white movie. The only thing missing was Cary Grant walking around the corner.

Elle paused a moment before stepping onto a large terrace. Steps cascaded down to a second and then a third terrace, all of which were bordered by sprawling lawns and gorgeous flower beds. The water stretched out below, with multiple docks extending into the bay.

Slowly, she took three steps and froze. The large orchestra decided just then to take a break, and it provided the exact right moment for every pair of eyes at the party to turn in her direction.

Oh. My. God.

Embarrassment coursed through her as her pulse picked up into a fast rhythm. Whispers carried up to her, causing her to consider running for the exit.

"Is that Ellie Owens?"

"Remember how she was in love with Jasper?"

"That's not Ellie. Ellie never looked like that."

"Remember that video she made?"

"Didn't she throw herself in the bay that night?"

She'd definitely wanted to make an impression. But Elle had been hoping that people would be dazzled by her dress as she talked to them one-on-one throughout the night. She had not planned to be the center of freaking attention. And where the hell was the orchestra?

As if on cue, Mrs. Dumont flicked a hand toward the conductor and he immediately began a new tune. Slowly, people returned to their drinks, food and conversations as Lilah Dumont, decked out in an elegant green gown glistening with gold beading, made her way toward Elle with open arms.

Elle allowed herself to be embraced as her hostess exclaimed, "Ellie, it's so good to see you. Welcome back!"

"Thank you for inviting me, Mrs. Dumont. Everything looks amazing."

"As do you." The older woman gave her a quick assessment. "You've certainly changed, Ellie."

"Oh, I go by Elle now."

With a soft pat to her cheek, Mrs. Dumont said, "Elle it is then. I'm sorry about what brought you home. Your dad is looking much better, though. He said he's in remission." A genuine smile touched the woman's lips.

Elle nodded. "Yes, his last doctor's appointment went well. But we'll have to make sure he stays on top of the situation. From everything I've read, this type of cancer can come back quickly. I'd like to meet his doctor," she added.

"He's the best oncologist in the state."

Realization dawned as she met Mrs. Dumont's gaze. "You helped, didn't you?"

Waving a hand in the air, Lilah winked at her. "It was

only a matter of a quick phone call. It also helps that a wing in that particular hospital is named after us."

What must it be like to have that kind of money? Elle wondered. She would be forever grateful. "Thank you so much. I don't know how to repay—"

"It was nothing. Now, if you'd really like to repay me you can do so by mingling and having fun."

Smiling, Elle nodded. Then she took a deep breath and made her way toward the other guests. As she walked across the patio, she spotted familiar faces—former classmates, teachers, local shop owners. Searching the crowd, she noticed her favorite art teacher and was about to say hi when a tall man wearing a tailored tux approached her.

"Ellie Owens?" he asked.

"Guilty," she replied. Taking a moment to place him, she finally remembered. "Tyler Briggitt! How are you?" They'd been in the same class in high school. Tyler had also been one of Jasper's closest friends.

"Great, no complaints. I'm working at the bank now. Welcome back. So," he began, "have you seen Jasp yet?"

She snagged a champagne flute from a passing waiter and took a fortifying sip. "Um, yeah. I ran into him yesterday, actually."

"That must have been awkward." Tyler leaned toward her, glanced to the right and then the left. Finally, he lowered his voice. "Remember that video?"

"Like it was yesterday," she said under her breath.

"That was some crazy stuff. Really bad."

"It certainly wasn't my finest moment." She tried to answer nonchalantly as Tyler turned to snag an appetizer off a nearby table. Maybe Cam had been onto something yesterday. After all, he'd tried to warn her that people didn't always forget the past.

"Man, I remember when they showed it at our senior prom—" Tyler began.

"It's so nice to see you again." Elle cut him off quickly. "But I see Riley Hudson over there and I'd really like to say hello. Have a great night."

Tyler didn't seem taken aback as Elle walked briskly toward Riley.

"Elle, hey." Riley waved when she spotted her.

"You look beautiful," she told the reporter. And she did. Riley was wearing a lavender chiffon gown with a low back. Long amethyst earrings dangled from her lobes and she'd accentuated her eyes with a soft lilac shadow.

"Thanks," Riley said brightly. "And you, wow. You look amazing. Red's a good color for you." She tipped her glass against Elle's in a toast. "Here's to two hot chicks and an incredible party." Elle took a huge sip as Riley added, "Are you having fun?"

"Um…" she began.

"Uh-oh, what's wrong?" True concern flashed in Riley's eyes.

How to explain? Elle knew she'd messed up senior year. But she'd thought that people would have enough class not to bring it up. Especially not the first person she talked to. Stupidly, she'd assumed that after ten years people would be interested in her life today as a sane, normal adult.

"I guess I was just hoping to blend in a bit more," she admitted quietly.

"Then, honey, you shouldn't have worn that dress." Riley's face softened. "Your return is the talk of the town. It'll die down."

God, she hoped that was true.

"But in the meantime…" Riley nudged her in the ribs with her elbow and Elle followed her stare across the terrace "…Jasper's right over there."

Now it was going to get weird. The whispers started up before she could even decide if she should walk over to greet him. Did no one remember anything else about her? What about her art? Or how she'd drawn that comic strip for the school newspaper? How she'd made the honor roll every single semester and eventually became valedictorian?

Well, she would have been valedictorian if the video had never come out. She could hear the principal's voice as if it had been yesterday.

"Ellie, your grades place you at the top of your class academically. But after that video... It just wouldn't be right."

Back in the present, her fate was decided when Jasper spotted her. He whispered something to the man he'd been chatting with, then headed toward her.

"I'll just let you two talk," Riley said, putting her champagne glass down on a table.

"No, Riley, wait," she said. But her old classmate was already walking away, waving at Jasper as she did.

Heat permeated every inch of Elle's skin as she felt all eyes on her and Jasper. Why had she wanted to come to this party? Her goal in being back in Bayside was to blend in, not stand out. And certainly to not make a fool out of herself or embarrass her father. Again.

"Ellie," he said, reaching for her wrist. "It's awesome you're here."

She couldn't help but notice that everyone around them was unabashedly watching her every move.

"Hi, Jasper," she said, squirming.

"Having fun?"

Not particularly. "It's great. Quite the turnout. Looks like the whole town is here." *Watching me. Judging me.*

"My parents' parties are always like this."

Something shifted and Elle reminded herself that she was an accomplished grown-up, not some shy bookworm who'd drunk too much one—and only one—night and paid a price for her bad choice. Let people watch the two of them talking. Nothing was going to happen. She'd make sure of that.

"I understand you took over your parents' company," she said, pushing her shoulders back and holding her head high.

A grin, fast and real, lit up his face. But quickly, interestingly, it faded. "Not yet. They're both still working pretty hard. But I'm in line to take over."

"I have to say I'm surprised."

His gaze dropped to the ground. "You and everyone else."

Feeling bad, she reached for his arm. "No, not like that. I only meant that I assumed Cam would take over, since he's older."

The statement appeared to placate Jasper and he reached for her fingers, squeezed then held on. Elle realized too late that she shouldn't have touched him. Nearby guests seemed to collectively hold their breath, and she could have sworn a flash went off.

She untangled her hand from his as he said, "Thanks, Elle. Yeah, my brother wanted to start his own company—much to our parents' disdain, especially Dad's. But there it is."

She wondered if Cam was here yet. Surely he would arrive soon. She wanted to hear more about his business and how he'd transitioned from Dumont golden boy to entrepreneur in his own right.

Jasper studied her for a moment, and she didn't know why, but she had the overwhelming urge to fidget.

"What?" she asked.

He shook his head. "Nothing. Sorry. It's just really nice to have you here."

For years she'd watched these parties from across the bay, desperately hoping to someday be in the very position she was in right now.

Yet it didn't feel like a dream come true. Jasper was nice enough, and of course he was beyond handsome. Still, something was missing. Or maybe someone…

Normally, Cam waited as long as possible before heading over to his parents' house for one of their dreaded parties. But tonight was different. He still hated putting on a tux and he really hated the mindless conversations he was about to endure, but there was a spring in his step that was usually absent.

"Someone got here nice and early. For a change," his mother called as he stepped onto the upper terrace. He gave her a quick hug, and when she pulled back, she smoothed a hand down his lapel. "You look dashing, Cameron."

Cam quirked an eyebrow. "Cameron, huh? Are we being formal tonight?"

Lilah Dumont chuckled. "Yes, you know our parties are always formal. Have you said hi to your father yet?"

"No need." Collin Dumont sauntered over, wrapped an arm around his wife and nodded briskly. "You're here early," he offered.

"So I've been told. What do I have to look forward to? Fireworks? A Ferris wheel? Dragons?"

"No, smart-ass," his mother said. She gestured toward a tray of champagne flutes, but Cam shook his head. He'd grab a beer later. "The most interesting thing tonight has been the arrival of Elle Owens."

Of course, Cam thought. "Where is she?" He found himself searching what felt like the population of the entire town to spot her. Poor girl probably needed someone to talk to. His gaze finally landed on the bottom terrace, where Elle stood in a dark red gown, her brown hair piled on top of her head. Even at a distance, her skin glowed, her dimples winked and that dress fitted her like a glove.

In a word, she looked stunning. His breath caught as she smiled.

Suddenly his stupid tie felt way too tight.

"They've been talking for the last twenty minutes or so," his mother added.

Cam shook his head and took a closer look at the situation. Elle was talking to none other than Jasper.

The man she'd been head over heels in love with back in high school. The guy who always got the girl. The brother Cam owed a huge debt of gratitude to.

"Nice for her to have a friend," he mumbled, and then quickly scanned the rest of the crowd. The usual suspects all seemed accounted for. But no matter how many times he tried to force his eyes away from her, he couldn't stop returning his gaze to Elle.

She laughed at something Jasper said and Cam could see that everyone around them was trying very ineffectively not to stare. Like goldfish being ogled in their bowl.

And did they have to stand so close to have a damn conversation? He shifted his weight and struggled with his tie again.

Jasper chose that moment to throw his head back and laugh. When he recovered, he stepped even closer. Gritting his teeth, Cam let out a gruff cough at the same time about ten flashes went off.

"Damn," he grumbled, as Elle and Jasper jumped apart. He could tell his brother tried to say something calming. But Elle ducked her head and retreated from the scene, leaving Jasper frowning into his champagne glass.

Cam's jaw ticked and he felt his hands curling into fists even as his mother was going on about something.

And why should Elle and Jasper bother him, anyway? It wasn't his problem. She wasn't his responsibility to watch over, and she certainly wasn't his girlfriend.

Yet he suddenly had an overwhelming desire to make

sure she was okay. Without another word to his mother, Cam took off.

It didn't take long to find her. He simply went in the opposite direction of the crowd, who were still talking in hushed tones about the reemergence of Ellie Owens.

"Elle?" he asked quietly.

She was standing under the gazebo at the edge of one of the gardens, looking out toward the bay. The twinkly lights illuminated her hair and accentuated the sparkles on her dress. When she turned toward him, Cam practically fell over.

She was absolutely breathtaking.

"Hi." The shy smile on her face fell the moment Cam neared.

"Not having the best night?" he guessed.

She didn't answer for a long moment. Finally, she sighed, a long, frustrated release of breath. "Not really."

From behind his back, he pulled out two bottles of beer. Her eyes lit up with interest. When he cocked his head, she nodded, and he proceeded to open them with the bottle opener he'd slipped into his pocket.

After a silent toast and clink of the bottles, she took a long pull then closed her eyes, looking content. Tentatively, he stepped closer. "May I?" he asked.

At her nod, he leaned on the railing and took in the view as he indulged in his own long pull of beer. They were quiet for a few minutes, enjoying the music of the band behind them and the gentle sound of water lapping in the nearby bay.

"You can barely see my house from here," she said, breaking the silence, her eyes trained out into the darkness. "I've been looking at your house from across the water most of my life."

"I was always jealous of your side of the bay. Really," he said at her skeptical glance. "You have neighbors and there were always picnics and barbecues happening over there. Our closest neighbor is acres away."

"Are you kidding? You have these lavish parties all the time. That's nothing compared to our lame barbecues."

"I'd much rather be flipping a burger than pretending to like caviar in front of my parents' clients."

"You don't like caviar?"

Cam was about to answer her when he realized she was joking. He leaned on the railing.

She brought the bottle to her lips and downed a good portion of the amber liquid. "What are you doing out here, anyway?"

"I came…" Why had he come after her? "I only wanted to…" What? What did he want?

She tilted her head, searched his face and waited.

"I figured you might need a friend."

Her eyes softened.

Cam threw back more beer. "And I like to hide during these things."

She laughed, and he decided he liked the way it made her face light up.

"I've never had any desire to be on a stage before," she told him. "Now I know why. I felt like everyone at this party was staring at me. I guess you were right to warn me yesterday."

Cam ran a hand over his face. He hadn't done a good job shaving on purpose. It drove his mother nuts when he didn't shave for one of her social functions. "For what it's worth, I would have rather been wrong. Besides, I've never liked people looking at me, either." He wasn't sure why he decided to tell Elle that.

She offered a half laugh. "I was under the impression you didn't like most things."

He grinned. "Not true. I just don't freely share my interests."

"What are your interests?"

He turned, leaned his back against the railing, swigged more beer. "Lots of things. Baseball, my truck, a cold beer on a hot day." He saluted her with his bottle. "I like working with my hands, always have. I like dogs and I'd like to get a puppy one of these days. I like a good book."

"What genre?" she asked.

"Thrillers mostly."

Mirroring his pose, she met his gaze as he told her about the last book he'd read. The next fifteen minutes passed as they talked about books, movies and television shows.

They finished their beers as a nice breeze filtered off the bay. It helped cool him down. When had he gotten so warm, anyway? But then he noticed her dainty shiver. Immediately, he removed his suit jacket and draped it around her shoulders without her asking.

Surprise flashed in her eyes. "Thanks," she said.

He shrugged. "You're cold. I gave you my jacket. That's how it works."

Tapping one of those sparkly fingers against her red lips, she admitted, "You were always kinda mysterious. No one knew much about you. You kept to yourself and drove a truck and had a beard."

"I didn't always have a beard."

"Felt like you did. During high school, you looked older than you were."

A fact that he'd used to his benefit whenever his friends wanted some cheap beer, he thought with a silent laugh.

Gazing at her now, with moonlight washing over, her eyes alight with amusement, her slender body swimming in his jacket, he thought he'd never seen any woman look so beautiful. He took a step closer. "So you really didn't know me at all."

Staying in place, she angled her head to look up at him. "Apparently not."

"How do you feel now that you are learning a little about me?" Was he flirting with her? Some part of his brain screamed for him to stop, but standing this close felt too damn good.

"I feel like I might be interested in hearing more."

And she was flirting back. Double damn. Elle Owens had been in love with his brother her entire life. Maybe Jasper hadn't been into her back in high school, but if what Cam witnessed earlier tonight was any indication, he was interested now. Cam would not, could not, interfere with his brother. Not after what his brother had done for him.

So he took a step back. And hated the way it made him feel.

"Jasper," he blurted out. She narrowed her eyes. "You and Jasper must have had a lot to talk about earlier."

He didn't miss her questioning look. Hell, he didn't blame her. He was running hot and cold.

"I don't really want to talk about Jasper."

"What do you want to talk about?"

She shrugged at first, but then she launched into what was really bothering her. "How is it that I've been gone for an entire decade, but tonight it felt like I'd been in Europe for ten days? People don't seem interested in learning who I am today."

"I don't know if that's true. You need to give it a little time. Your return is a big deal in this small town."

"I don't know how many more nights like this I can endure."

"If it makes you feel better, I liked who you were back then. And so far, I like who you are today."

Her mouth opened and closed. "You aren't like everyone else."

"Yeah, I've gotten that my whole life."

She giggled.

"Listen, you've changed a lot since you were eighteen.

You're beautiful, smart—hell, you've lived in Europe. But you've been gone for ten years. People are interested."

"You think I'm beautiful?"

The amazement he heard in her voice pissed him off. How could she not know she was stunning? Wasn't it obvious? It seemed so to him. Even if she hadn't been wearing that hot red dress... His mind went to a very dark, but very happy place at the idea of her not wearing a dress.

He stepped toward her once again, invading her personal space. "You don't think so?" It was a challenge, but he didn't know why. Only that he needed her to get it.

"I happen to think I'm very pretty. But I also know I haven't always been."

To her credit, she didn't back off. Impressive, since Cam knew he was physically intimidating.

"So what?"

"So people in this town only see the drunk girl in that video professing her love for someone who was way out of her league."

Cam slapped his hands down on the railing on either side of her, boxing her in. "The people of this town are idiots."

She continued to hold her ground, tilting her head up to meet his gaze. "But you're not."

"I don't generally call myself an idiot, no."

"You're telling me that you look at me now and you don't see young, sweet, if misguided, Ellie Owens?"

"I'm looking at you right now and what I see is a smoking-hot, stubborn woman with thick hair and shining eyes and smooth, silky skin." He emphasized this by running a hand up and down her arm. Despite still wearing his jacket, she shivered, and he moved even closer.

His eyes locked on to her red lips. When her tongue slipped out to moisten them, he almost groaned. He raised his other hand to the side of her face. Wanting to kiss her more than he wanted to breathe, Cam began to lean down. His lips hovered a hairbreadth from hers.

Then a loud explosion sounded, followed by a round of applause and cheers. Jumping back, he ran a hand through his hair, as Elle looked up at the fireworks lighting the sky above them.

The moment was ruined, but Cam knew they'd been saved from making what would have clearly been a horrible mistake.

He usually felt grateful at such times. Weird thing was, tonight he felt nothing but disappointment.

Chapter Five

Am I the only one who saw a gorgeous Ellie Owens enter the *Printemps* party like a princess? The really exciting part was when Ellie and everyone's favorite hunk, Jasper, finally rendezvoused on the terrace for over twenty minutes, if my calculations were correct. (A watch didn't fit with my outfit.)

New-couple alert? Not quite yet. Our Cinderella left Prince Charming holding his imported champagne, and disappeared for the rest of the night. Of course, yours truly has an idea as to where she went. Didn't anyone else notice the other major player who was missing from the party...?

The following evening, Elle walked into the Boat House, one of Bayside's nicer restaurants, located on the water. Riley had texted her early that morning, stating they needed a postparty recap.

Wearing a chic black jumpsuit with large emerald jewelry, Riley was already seated at a high table in the bar area, furiously scribbling away in a reporter's notebook.

They made quick work of ordering their drinks. Elle got a glass of pinot noir and Riley decided on a pomegranate martini.

"What are you working on?" Elle asked, nodding toward Riley's notes.

"This article that's been plaguing me. My stupid boss wants more articles on the food scene." Riley made air quotes at the idea. "We live in Bayside, not New York. There's not really a food scene here."

Elle sat back and studied her friend. Riley dressed like she was on a trendy television show and talked about New York constantly. "You seem to really love big cities."

Riley nodded. "I did. I do," she said, quickly correcting herself.

"So why didn't you move to one after school?"

She chuckled. "Are you trying to get rid of me already? We just became friends."

Elle blushed. "I didn't mean it that way."

Waving a hand in the air, Riley didn't look the least bit affected. "I'm kidding." The drinks arrived and she took a sip of her martini. "I went to NYU and stayed in Manhattan after college."

"Really?" Interested, Elle took a sip of her wine. Good, but not quite like a glass in Florence. Table wine in Italy was better than expensive bottles in the United States. "Why did you come back?"

Riley's clear green eyes clouded at the question. Her entire demeanor changed and she quickly looked down at the table. "Let's just say that I went to New York with a goal to conquer the city." She twisted the cocktail napkin that had come with her drink. "In the end, the city conquered me."

Nodding as if she understood, even though she definitely wanted to hear more, Elle decided to change the subject. "So, did you have a good time last night?"

Riley smiled. "I did. Didn't see much of you, though. After you talked to Jasper, that is."

Sitting up straight, Elle said, "Oh, I didn't do anything with Jasper, if that's what you mean."

"I didn't think you had." Riley took another sip of her drink.

She knew Riley was probing, and ordinarily she wasn't into gossip. But it was so refreshing to have a friend to gossip with, Elle let her guard down. "I was talking to Cam for a long time, actually."

Riley's eyebrows shot up. "Cam Dumont? Seriously?"

It dawned on Elle that she'd spoken more to Cam in the last three days than she had in her first eighteen years. Just as she'd told him last night, he was mysterious. Always had been. But now that she was older, that ambiguity intrigued rather than intimidated her. When she spoke with him, it felt like he was really listening to her, absorbing her words, adding his own thoughts. She'd stayed with him for an hour and the time seemed to fly by. When he'd stepped closer to her, she'd reveled in his nearness, become excited about what might happen.

Shrugging at Riley's question, Elle took a long gulp of her drink. "Is that so surprising?"

"Well, yeah. Cam's a nice guy, but he isn't the, um, biggest conversationalist in Bayside." Riley sat back and tapped a manicured finger against her lips. "That must be who the Bayside Blogger was talking about in her post this morning."

"You're kidding, right?" Elle took a quick glance around the room. Was that blogger here now, hidden among the patrons?

"You made the top of her article today. She said you had disappeared from the party, but so had someone else, although she didn't say who it was. I didn't even think about Cam."

Narrowing her eyes, Elle leaned forward. "What do you know about him?"

"Oh, jeez, not much. Cam keeps to himself. He's friendly enough, always says hi to me. Wait a minute..." Riley copied Elle's posture. "Do you like Cam?"

Elle rolled her eyes. "Check yes, no or maybe?"

"Okay, let me rephrase. Are you interested in Cam?"

"I just got back to town. I'm still jet-lagged." Riley

nailed her with a pointed gaze, but Elle tried to hold firm. "Besides, I'm not interested in anyone, most certainly not a Dumont brother."

The truth was, she wanted to know more about Cam. But what she emphatically didn't want to do was cause more gossip to come her way by switching from one brother to the other. Of course, that would imply she'd actually been with one brother before, which she obviously had not.

Luckily, Riley forgot about the Dumont brothers and the two of them moved on to discussing the different gowns at the party. After that, they talked about Florence, and Elle filled Riley in on the last art gallery she'd worked at before coming home.

"What are you thinking for work now that you're home?" Riley asked, as they enjoyed their second drinks of the night.

Elle blew a wayward hair out of her eye. "That's the big question. The types of jobs I'm qualified for, like gallery work, don't really exist here."

Riley looked pensive for a moment before snapping her fingers. "Maybe you can teach art in a school?"

She'd thought of that herself. "I would probably enjoy that, but unfortunately, I don't have my teaching certification, so I'd have to go back to school for it. And I'll need some source of income soon. I'm not opposed to waitressing."

"You can't come back from your glamorous life in Italy only to waitress in Bayside. There has to be something else we can find for you."

"Well, this looks like trouble."

They both glanced up to see Jasper, wearing khaki pants and a mint-green polo, a light-colored jacket thrown over his arm, strolling over to them. He leaned against the table, acknowledged Riley, then turned his attention completely to Elle. Once again, she felt every pair of eyes in the place swivel in her direction.

"What are the two most beautiful women in Bayside talking so intensely about?"

Elle couldn't miss the interested way Riley watched them.

"We were discussing what kind of job Elle should go after," Riley informed him.

"You can always come work for me," he said quickly.

Elle's cheeks were heating up under the intense stare from Jasper, the attention of the whole bar, or both. "That's a really nice offer," she said, scooting her chair away from the table. "But I'm not suited to real estate."

"My parents think I'm not, either."

It was a small comment, fast in delivery, and said with a smile. Yet Elle perked up at it, her heart going out to him and the way that smile didn't quite meet his eyes.

"I'm sorry." Lame as far as responses went, but it was all she could think to say.

"Why don't the two of you have dinner with me?" Jasper suggested hopefully.

"Oh, um… I'm not really dressed for dinner." Elle motioned to the tight black pants and plum top she wore.

"Are you kidding? You look great. Riley, you in?" Jasper's eyes lit up.

"Let's do it." Riley popped up off her chair and followed Jasper to the hostess station.

What would her dad think of Elle having dinner with Jasper? Would he even find out? Would the Bayside Blogger? Was the mysterious writer here right now?

Elle shook her head. She was being ridiculous and paranoid. Dinner with Jasper and Riley would be fun. Plus, with Riley there, how much gossip could come out of the evening? Would the Bayside Blogger care if she ordered the scallops or the crab cake? Unlikely.

She took the seat Jasper held out for her at a table near the window overlooking the bay. They ordered drinks and Jasper asked Riley how things were going at the paper. As she filled him in, Elle did a quick check of the restaurant. No one seemed to be paying them any attention at the moment.

Thank God. Elle finally sat back and took a long drink of water. Just as she'd hoped, with Riley at the table, chattering away, everyone must have understood that this dinner was nothing more than three friends—well, sort of—having dinner together.

Riley's phone let out a little chirp and she reached for it. "Oh, sorry, it's Sawyer."

"Her boss," Jasper explained.

"Oh, right, she mentioned him the other day."

Riley's eyebrows pulled together and her mouth puckered as she read the text.

"Everything okay?" Elle asked, finally relaxing enough to sit back comfortably in her seat.

Shaking her head, Riley let out a huff. "No. I swear, Sawyer Wallace is driving me nuts. One of these days I'm going to throw him right in the bay."

Jasper let out a laugh. "That will be interesting. Make sure and give me advanced warning so I can be there with my camera."

"Oh, I will." She put her cell phone in her purse and turned to Elle with pleading eyes. "I'm so sorry, but I have to go back to the office."

Nooo! Elle sat up straight. "Are you sure? Is everything okay?"

"Sawyer has an issue with one of my stories. It's set to run tomorrow and we're on deadline. The man can't do anything over the phone or email. I'm sorry," she repeated to Jasper.

"That's a bummer," he said. "Tell Sawyer I said he owes you a full dinner and drinks."

"Don't worry, I won't let him forget he ruined my plans." Riley rose and turned to Elle again. "I really am sorry, but please try to have fun."

Elle smothered the large frustrated sigh she wanted to let out. "Of course. And if everything gets worked out quickly, come on back."

"Yeah, we'll save you dessert," Jasper offered.

"Thanks, guys." With that, Riley took her exit and Elle and Jasper were alone.

As they mulled over the menu, Elle couldn't help but glance around the room, constantly noticing person after person turning to watch them.

Once his scotch arrived, they gave their orders to the waiter and Elle settled back in her chair. Jasper immediately started chatting about some of the recent happenings around town.

She watched him as he talked. He was so handsome, she couldn't help thinking. His looks were reminiscent of an old-Hollywood actor. Golden hair and light eyes, tall and lean. Not to mention he was wealthy, well educated and came from a great family.

And yet she didn't feel that little pull. That tingling feeling of awareness she usually got when she was attracted to someone. That feeling she used to get when she was around him back in high school.

That feeling she'd experienced last night as she stood under the gazebo with his brother.

Now, there was something to think about. But luckily, Jasper unknowingly saved her from having to deal with that acknowledgment when he began asking her questions about her time in Florence.

A short while later, she was digging into the stuffed flounder dish she'd ordered.

"Did you ever study abroad?" she asked as he finished questioning her about Italy. She still didn't feel any kind of spark, but she had to admit he was a good conversationalist.

He shook his head. "Unfortunately, I never had time."

Cocking her head, she asked, "What do you mean?"

"Let's just say that I went off to college and was very focused." He stretched both hands out in front of him. "I had a goal and nothing was going to deter me from reaching it."

Interesting, she thought. Elle would have imagined his college days would be filled with frat parties and road trips. After all, he'd been the most popular kid in school.

"What did you major in?"

"Business. What else?" He grinned. "Then I got my MBA."

He went on to describe some of the jobs he'd held both during and after earning his MBA. Impressed, Elle had to admit there was more to Jasper than she'd thought.

"And now you're being groomed to take over the family business." She said it with a smile, but when she saw the shadows pass over Jasper's face, her smile faltered. "You okay?" she asked.

He shrugged. "I'm fine. I wouldn't say I'm being groomed so much as being used for a placeholder."

"What does that mean?"

"My parents are still hoping Cam will come back."

She opened her mouth to protest, but Jasper held up a hand to stop her.

"I love my parents and they have a lot of amazing traits. But one thing I'll never get is how much stock they put into these antiquated ideas. Martinis before dinner, no social media, oldest son takes over the company."

Elle bit her lip. "I'm sure most of it's generational."

"Maybe. But if they want Dumont Incorporated to have

a fighting chance in this generation, they need to start evolving."

"Have you talked to them about it?"

"I've talked. They've yelled. I've tried again. They've rolled their eyes." He reached for his scotch, then realized his glass was empty. Looking up, he didn't quite meet her eyes. "But enough about that." He grinned. "First-world problems, right?"

"Maybe," she agreed. "But they're still important problems to you."

Now he did meet her eyes. "Thanks, Elle. You know, if I wasn't da—"

A flash went off and they both turned in that direction, to find a table of women unabashedly watching them. All three held cell phones in their hands. Elle looked to the left and noticed two more tables of people observing them.

She sat back and shook her head. Jasper raised an eyebrow.

"Doesn't it bother you?" she asked.

"What?" he said with a blank stare. "People assuming we're on a date?"

"Exactly. I don't want to be the center of attention."

She'd been a quiet, serious teenager. Except for her stupid crush on Jasper. A crush, she'd learned tonight, that had been based on nothing concrete. Because the Jasper she'd just finished having dinner with was nice and sweet and very smart. But he wasn't her soul mate. She didn't feel attracted to him at all. In fact, what she felt was sorry that he was going through a rough time with his parents.

After the party last night and dinner now, Elle could truly say that she really never knew the real Jasper Dumont, and she had to wonder if anyone else did, either.

At this realization, she sat up straighter, then folded her napkin and placed it on the table. "I know we haven't ordered dessert yet, but would you mind if we got out of here?"

His face softened. "Absolutely." He signaled the waiter for their check. "And, Ellie?"

She looked up.

"I meant Elle," he said with a grin. "Thanks for listening tonight."

"Anytime. And I mean that."

Once the bill was paid and they were outside the restaurant, Jasper turned to her. "How did you get here?" he asked.

"My dad dropped me off, actually. Kind of like high school." She smiled. "I don't have my own car yet."

"Let me drive you home," he offered.

"Actually, it's nice to be in the fresh air. I think I'll walk off that yummy dinner. But thank you."

Jasper replaced his keys in his pocket and zipped up his jacket. "Then you have to let me walk you. Maybe you'll even let me in on what happened back there." He nudged his shoulder against hers.

They began heading toward the path that led around the bay.

"I don't want to make a mistake, I guess. And certainly not while everyone's watching me."

He exhaled and then stopped at one of the overlooks that offered a great view of the water and harbor. "That's how I feel every single day at work."

She raised an eyebrow. "Come on. You're a Dumont. Your name is on the stationery," she teased. But he didn't smile.

"It's kind of a lot of pressure to have your name everywhere."

Turning her head, she took in his expression. It was strange to see this serious side of Bayside's golden boy. Unsure what to say to make him feel better, she leaned against the railing while she considered. The metal barrier squeaked and rocked. It was loose. Elle took a step back.

She could see the wheels turning in his head, even as he grabbed her fingers and squeezed. "Anyway, don't let me ruin our night. We had a great dinner."

"Excuse me? Dinner?" This came from a voice that happened to sound both high-pitched and unhappy.

Elle and Jasper turned around. A pretty woman, petite, with blond hair and well-tailored clothes, approached them.

"Never mind the dinner, what in the hell are you doing holding hands with a beautiful woman?" she asked, her eyes trained on Jasper.

He edged away from Elle and held up his hands in front of him in surrender. "What are you doing home?"

The woman took a step closer. "I came home a day early to surprise you. Looks like I did more than that."

Feeling beyond awkward, Elle coughed lightly. "I think you have the wrong impression." The other woman crossed her arms over her chest and shot her an oh-really-please-tell-me expression. "We went to high school together and we were only catching up. I'm Elle," she said. "Elle Owens."

"Mindy Peterson. Jasper's girlfriend."

Oh, crap. A myriad of emotions filtered through Elle and she had no idea which one to hone in on. Jasper had a girlfriend? As she continued standing there like an idiot, head bobbing back and forth as she looked from Jasper to Mindy, she felt dumber than ever, and that made the anger come.

"You have a girlfriend?" she said, her voice coming out louder than she'd intended.

"Unbelievable." Mindy shook her own head, her perfect blond hair cascading around her like she was in a shampoo commercial. "He didn't tell you about me? What the hell, Jasp?"

Mindy took another step toward Jasper and Elle figured that was her cue to leave. She mumbled something about heading home, but neither seemed to hear her. So she turned to go, remembering too late that her back had been to the water and the rickety railing.

Before she could stop the inevitable, or even let out a scream, Elle was falling into the bay.

Chapter Six

Who was spotted at the Boat House this evening? None other than little Ellie Owens and Jasper Dumont, at the most romantic table at the restaurant. Wanna know more deets? Come chat with me on Twitter...

Elle could definitely swim, but while she was under the still-cold-from-the-winter water, she considered staying under the surface indefinitely. There was no way she wanted to face Jasper and Mindy after falling into the bay.

Or anyone.

Ever again.

As she began making her way to the top, she realized that her clothes were weighing her down. Panic overtook her and she started to flail her arms and legs. But no sooner had she started squirming than she felt a pair of strong arms encircle her middle securely and propel her upward.

Surfacing, she spit water out of her mouth, gave a couple coughs and pushed her hair from her face. Twisting, she came face-to-face with a handsome chin covered with dark stubble and glistening drops of water.

Cam Dumont had come to her rescue.

"Are you okay?" he asked, trying to grab hold of her again. She remained quiet, more out of embarrassment than anything else. But he must have taken her silence for shock or injury. "Elle? Talk to me. Are you okay?" he repeated, as they bobbed up and down in the frigid bay.

"Cam, do you have her? Is she okay?" Jasper's voice filtered down from the overlook above them.

"Elle?" Cam tried again. He ran a hand over her face before grabbing her to him, pressing her wet body against his rock-hard abs and pecs. She couldn't help but think if she was about to die of embarrassment, being smothered against Cam's body wasn't the worst way to go.

"I'm fine," she finally mumbled against his chest.

"What was that?" His worried voice washed over her.

"I'm okay," she said loudly, out of breath from treading water.

"No, you're not okay. Why did you do that?"

Huh? Do what?

Cam's lips were starting to turn blue. She could imagine how hers looked.

He fisted his hands in her shirt, bringing her to him. "I love him, but trust me, Jasper's not worth it."

What a weird statement.

She pushed away from him. "I can swim. Let's get out of here." With a couple big kicks, she began to make her way to the edge of the water. Cam helped her up and over the supporting wall and then hoisted himself over, as well.

He reached for her again, his eyes searching, looking over every inch of her. Then he pulled her into a tight hug. "Jesus, you made my heart stop."

Wow, he really seemed worried. Falling into the frigid water of the bay at night wasn't exactly her idea of a good time, but it was as if she'd done it on purp...

That's when it dawned on her. Cam thought she'd thrown herself in the water on purpose. "Oh, no," she said quickly. "I fell in accidentally."

Elle's pulse started pounding a mile a minute. Flashbacks to the night of her dreaded senior prom slammed into her brain. As if that stupid video hadn't been bad enough, she'd fled the gym and run home. Only someone had called her name, and when she'd turned, her foot had slipped and into the bay she went. That had been an accident, as well, only no one had believed her. They all thought she'd been so upset over Jasper that she'd thrown herself in.

Ridiculous. She would never attempt to get attention that way. Only a crazy person would. But as she began to see the crowd forming on the overlook, she quickly realized that she was close to being labeled a crazy person once more.

She pushed back from Cam and met his gaze. "I swear. I turned to leave and didn't realize where I was standing, and the railing over there is loose. Someone should fix that. You're in construction. Maybe you can do it." She was fully aware that she was rambling but his expression hadn't changed. If nothing else, she didn't want anyone to think she'd thrown herself in on purpose. And most definitely not Cam Dumont.

"This was an accident?" he asked, disbelief clouding his voice.

"I swear."

She wanted to say more, but at that moment Jasper, Mindy and a whole bunch of other people came running down the embankment.

"Is she okay?" Mindy asked.

"Elle, are you okay?" Jasper asked, reaching them. "You're shivering." He ran his hands up and down her arms. "Jesus, you're freezing."

Mindy slapped his arm. "Give her your coat."

Jasper looked down at his expensive jacket and then took in her soaking-wet body. Before he had to decide if her possible hypothermia was worth it, a soft jacket was being draped around her shoulders. Cam pulled his flannel coat around her tightly, zipping up the front. He must have shed the jacket before he jumped in the water. He rubbed his hands up and down her arms, even as the crowd around them continued to grow.

"I'm sorry, Elle," Mindy said. "I got the wrong impression back there."

"'S 'kay." She ground out the reply through teeth that were now chattering.

Elle wanted to melt into the ground, and only half of it had to do with the heat Cam's capable hands were generating. Hearing the hushed, but excited whispers in the crowd, Elle knew without a doubt that everyone was assuming she'd done yet another foolish thing to win over Jasper.

Humiliation flushed her cheeks even as her teeth rattled together.

"Elle, what happened?" Riley asked, elbowing her way through the crowd.

"I'm…fine…nothing…to…worry…about…"

"I saw everything," someone in the ever-growing crowd said. "She fought with Jasper and then went overboard."

"No, Jasper's girlfriend pushed her over," someone else offered.

"Jasper Dumont has a girlfriend?" another person asked incredulously.

Elle sneezed once, twice, three times in rapid succession.

"Enough," Cam called out. "I'm getting her home. Now."

With that, he picked her up. If she wasn't so busy dying of mortification, she would totally swoon at the ease with which he lifted her. Instead, she snuggled into his chest and closed her eyes.

Next thing she knew, Cam had set her in his truck, turned the key in the ignition and was blasting the cab with heat. Then he walked to the driver's-side door and stripped. Just tore his top off right there in the community parking lot. His pants went next.

Wow. Don't need a heater anymore.

Cam got into the car wearing nothing but a pair of wet boxer briefs. Wet and very snug black boxer briefs.

After closing his door, he leaned over and framed her face in his hands. He looked deeply into her eyes. "Do I need to take you to a hospital?"

Elle froze. Cam was touching her and he wasn't wearing any clothes.

And he looked good. Damn good.

"You're naked," she squeaked. As soon as the words left her mouth she wanted to get out of the car and throw herself back in the bay.

A cocky grin appeared, lighting up his eyes with mischief for a second. One second. Then his usual serious expression returned. "I'll take that as a no."

"Why did you take your clothes off?"

"You seem to be distracted by my nakedness. That means you're not thinking about how you just pitched yourself over the railing and into the freezing water." He turned one of the vents in his direction and the blast of air made his wet, curly hair blow.

"Excuse me? I did not." She pointed over her shoulder in the general direction of the dock. "Tell me you don't think I did that for attention."

He shrugged and stayed silent.

Huffing out a breath, she pulled his jacket around her tighter. "The railing is loose and when Mindy showed up, I figured she and Jasper probably needed some alone time, so I turned to leave. I guess I'd lost track of how close to the railing I was standing and... Why am I defending myself to you?"

He quirked an eyebrow.

"Seriously, Cam. You are so annoying."

He threw his head back and laughed. The movement

did interesting things to his solid body. "Put some damn clothes on already," she yelled.

The laughing stopped but the smile remained. More like a smirk, but still… "I don't have any extra clothes and I'm not putting on those wet ones and dying of pneumonia."

"Fine." She turned to the window as he put the truck into Drive. "What were you doing down there, anyway?"

"It's Saturday night. I was going to have a beer with a friend of mine. Saw you, ahem, meet Mindy, and then go into the water."

She whipped around. "That's another thing. You could have given me a heads-up about Jasper's girlfriend."

Elle felt Cam stiffen next to her. Maybe it had been a passing headlight, but she also noticed that a shadow fell over his face. "Must have been awkward."

"A bit. I mean, I wouldn't have had dinner with him—"

The car swerved. "You had dinner with my brother?"

"It's not like it was a date. Riley was with us until she got called back to work. It was just one little dinner."

"Probably wasn't so little to Mindy."

Elle felt awful. She would never, ever, ever go out with someone else's boyfriend. Ever.

"The whole town saw that go down. Didn't they?" she asked quietly.

He turned and gave her a long once-over before returning his gaze to the road in front of him. "Yep."

"Well, isn't that just peachy. Looks like I stepped off the plane from Italy and walked right back into the past."

"Elle…" he began. But he didn't say anything else.

Leaning her head against the seat rest, she closed her eyes and willed the entire last couple days to be a dream. From the *Printemps* party with all the looks, stares and whispers, to dinner with Jasper and meeting his girlfriend, to the damn Bayside Blogger, Elle wanted a do-over in a big way.

"I've said it before but I'm going to say it again. I'm glad you're back," Cam said in his rough, yet massively appealing voice.

His words struck her deeply. Because the only thing she wouldn't change from the last couple days was sitting right next to her.

"Hey, Cam." She kept her eyes closed. "Not that I needed it, but thanks for saving me tonight."

Sunday was Cam's one day off. As such, it was typically spent sleeping in, being lazy, watching whatever sporting event was in season and generally relaxing.

So why, then, could he not seem to chill out and decompress like every other Sunday?

Maybe because he didn't usually spend his Saturday nights jumping into the cold-as-hell bay rescuing gorgeous women.

Or maybe it had to do with the memory of said gorgeous woman's wet body plastered against his.

During the car ride to Elle's house, he'd caught her eyeing him. Her interest had made his body react in ways that were completely inappropriate for confined spaces. And pantless men.

"Damn, Elle," he mumbled as he flicked through the channels on his big screen. He'd been through all two million channel options only a total of ten times already. There was nothing he wanted to see, except maybe Elle's face when he'd removed his clothes.

Yeah. That hadn't been so bad.

He rose and circled the room, trying to figure out what would make him feel less restless. The fact that Elle's face kept popping into his mind only served to irritate him more.

Like the rest of the town, he'd been quick to assume

that she'd pitched herself into the inky, black water. And he could tell how much his assumption had cost her.

But was she still into Jasper? Cam shook his head. Hell if he could figure out what she was thinking. All he knew was that he was having a bunch of inappropriate thoughts about a woman who had once been seriously into his baby brother.

But Elle truly didn't seem as interested as everyone thought. And neither did Jasper. Which meant…maybe Cam could step into the ring.

He ran a hand over his hair. Damn if he didn't want to see her again. Would that be so wrong?

Guilt coiled in his chest, but that guilt went to war with the desire curling in other areas. Even if he knew how to get in her good graces…

Actually, he knew just the thing.

Picking up his cell, he punched in a number, a grin spreading on his face. Not long after that phone call, Cam made the short drive to Elle's father's house. He'd spent a lot of time at this house when Ted was sick, fixing odd things here and there and planting some flowers and stuff around the porch.

Those flowers currently looked like they were blooming, and he mentally patted himself on the back. Hopping up on the porch, he was about to knock when he heard raised voices coming from the back of the small house. Elle and her dad must be in the kitchen. Silently, he pulled open the screen door and walked inside.

"I swear, Dad. For the hundredth time, I did not purposely throw myself into the water." Ted must have said something in reply but Cam didn't catch it. Then Elle retorted, "I didn't do it in high school, either. I promise you the railing was wobbly."

Ted Owens coughed. "The Bayside Blogger reported—"

A low groan sounded from Elle. "Please don't tell me

you read that crap, too. Come on, Daddy. You know me. Don't you?" she asked after a pause.

Deciding to save her, Cam revealed himself. "She's not lying." Two sets of very similar green eyes turned in his direction. "The railing was loose."

Was being the operative word. After he'd delivered Elle to her worried and obviously upset father, a nearly naked Cam took a hot shower, redressed and then returned to the scene of the crime, where he'd quickly secured the railing with the help of the large lantern he kept in his truck for night jobs.

After he'd seen the evidence for himself, he realized she'd been telling the truth all along.

"Cam," Elle said in surprise. "What are you doing here?"

"I... Hey, it smells really good." That's when he noticed the pots on the stove, the plates, napkins and silverware set on the table, and the apron tied tightly around Elle's narrow waist.

"Ellie's cooking dinner tonight." Cam spotted the quick look of pride Ted shot toward his daughter before he set his features into a hard expression again. "And you," he started, pointing a finger at Cam.

Even with many inches in height and considerably more muscle than the guy, Cam backed up. There was nothing like a father protecting his daughter. His beautiful, vulnerable daughter, whose head was currently tilted as she watched him with interest.

"What did I do?" Cam asked from the corner.

Elle bit down on a smile and mixed something in a pot.

"You dropped my daughter off wearing nothing but your underwear."

"He was cold, Daddy," Elle unhelpfully offered with a grin as she placed large hunks of mozzarella cheese and thick slices of tomato on a plate with some green leafy thing.

"Then you'd think some clothes would help out."

Cam cringed. Being naked in the truck with Elle probably hadn't given off the best message. Still, he had pulled her out of the water. "I am not the villain here. I'm the good guy."

"That's up for debate," Elle said under her breath.

"I saved her."

"I don't need saving," she said, looking indignant as she wielded a bottle of balsamic vinegar. "And if I ever do need saving, I can do it myself."

"Oh, yeah," Cam said, walking around Ted and aiming a disbelieving look at her. "Like you did last night. Hmm, was that before or after you fell into the damn water?"

Ted took a seat at the table and crossed one leg over the other. Not attempting to hide an amused look, he sat back and observed the two of them.

"That. Was. An. Accident." Her face was dewy from the steam coming off the pots on the stove. Cam thought she looked appealing as all get-out. She drained water from a pot and then quickly threw the contents into another pan, mixing everything together.

"We're only looking out for you, princess."

"Yeah," Cam added. And when had that started? he wondered.

"Excuse me." Elle hip-bumped Cam—hard—and continued assembling the meal. She lifted the pan, her muscles straining as she dished the contents onto a large platter. "I didn't realize I had two dads now," she said to Cam, mirroring his thoughts. "When did you start monitoring every little thing I do?"

"I, uh…"

"Daddy," Elle said, with a nod to the platter. Dutifully, Ted put the food on the table. "Cameron, make yourself useful," she said, handing him a large bowl of salad and a basket of bread to put there, as well.

A moment later, she had untied her apron and both Elle and Ted were sitting at the table. "Are you going to sit down or what?" she asked.

"Ellie," Ted warned. "Manners."

"Sorry." She looked up at Cam. "Oh, hero extraordinaire, would you like to join us for dinner? It would truly be our honor."

Cam was taken aback. He hadn't come over for a free dinner, although it smelled so good, he definitely didn't want to pass on it. "I, uh, didn't even bring anything."

"You've done plenty," Ted said. Then he turned to his daughter, who had perked up at the statement. "Cam came by almost every day while I was going through treatment. He really helped out around here."

Elle studied Cam, her eyes softening. "Thank you. That means a lot to me."

Touched at the sudden emotion pouring from her, he quickly made a joke. "Hey, if I knew I would get some home-cooked meals out of the deal, I would have done a lot more."

Comfortable conversation passed between them as they ate. There was no further mention of the bay, Jasper or what had transpired the night before.

"I didn't know you could cook." Cam took his last bite. "This was really delicious." He meant it. Elle *was* a good cook. Another point for her.

When had he started keeping track?

"There's a lot you don't know about me, and thanks." She tried to cover up a proud smile, but he'd caught it.

"So I guess now that you've fed me I should come clean and tell you the real reason I came by."

Elle tilted her head in a way identical to her father. Cam stifled a grin.

"Not to see if I was okay?" she asked.

"I can see that you are. Actually, I have a job offer for you."

Ted put down his fork, an attentive expression on his face. Folding her hands together, Elle rested her chin on them. "What kind of job?"

"Nothing permanent, unfortunately. I'm doing a renovation for an old high school friend. She's pregnant with twins and wants a real fancy nursery with the works. She's been looking for someone to paint a floor-to-ceiling mural in the designated room, but hasn't found anyone she likes." He took a sip of the wine Elle had put out for dinner. "I said you were into that kind of stuff."

"And she just hired me based on you telling her about me?" Elle's eyes were huge.

"I vouched for you."

"I can't believe you thought about helping me find a job," she said, awe lacing her voice.

"You mentioned you didn't know what you were going to do for work."

A huge smile blossomed on her face and made Cam smile in return. "I can't even begin to thank you enough."

Embarrassed, he shrugged. "It was nothing."

Ted got up, patted Cam on the back. "It's something. I'll let you two talk over the details." With that, he walked toward the living room, carrying his glass of wine.

"It's short notice. But you start tomorrow morning. I can pick you up on my way over. Carson, my friend, does want to see some samples of your work, so I hope you have something you can show her."

Elle nodded. "Seriously, this is so awesome of you."

She covered his hand with her own and Cam felt a jolt all the way down to his toes. All he could do was stare into her eyes. Those deep, fascinating eyes.

Instinctively, he laced their fingers together. He couldn't

remember the last time he'd held hands with a female. Never much cared for it. But it felt good with Elle. It felt... different.

"What color are your eyes?"

She'd been eyeing their joined hands, but looked back up at his question. "What?" She laughed. "Um, green."

"No." He shook his head. "They're too pretty to be just green."

A blush tinted her cheeks. "Thanks."

"Ellie," her father called from the other room. Like two teenagers making out, they both pushed back from the table, yanking their hands apart. "Do we have any more of this wine?"

Laughing lightly, she stood up. "You don't need any more." She turned from the table and froze. "How pretty. Look." She pointed out the window.

Cam didn't need to look to know what she was talking about. The sunset over the bay was amazing most nights. Tonight, however, it was extraordinary. Blurring shades of orange, red, yellow and pink were reflecting off the water, making it seem like there were two sunsets instead of just one. The changing light highlighted Elle's hair, casting a glow around her.

"The dishes can wait. Come here." She slipped out the sliding doors that led to their tiny deck.

Following, he shoved his hands in his pockets as she leaned on the railing. "Careful," he teased. "Railings tend to fall around here."

"Aren't you clever," she answered in a dry voice.

Holding in a chuckle, he focused on the peaceful sunset instead. Minutes passed as they stood together in comfortable silence, watching the sky change colors.

He liked being around Elle. Most women wanted to talk about their feelings. Not that there was anything wrong with that when it was needed. But there was a lot to be said for enjoying a quiet moment.

Plus, she could hold her own with him.

And she could cook.

And she was gorgeous.

Sneaking a glance at her, he felt his heart practically stop. She'd let her hair out of its ponytail. Now the wind was moving through it, light brown strands flying around her face. The setting sun cast an aura over her that highlighted her smooth skin. Awash in light, with a dreamy expression on her face, she looked serene, calm. Exquisite.

Exquisite? Ah, hell. He liked her.

"Damn."

She turned her head at his oath. "What was that?" she asked, an amused expression on her face.

He couldn't like her. Not if she had any feelings for his brother. That wouldn't be right.

All he wanted to do was kiss her. With his body tensed and primed at her nearness, he desperately wanted to draw her to him. He wanted those lips on his, those arms around him.

"Cam?"

He met her curious gaze. Why couldn't she be weird or crazy or just not his type?

"What are you thinking?" she wondered aloud.

"Do you still have feelings for my brother?" he blurted. Idiot. Her face fell and then he cursed himself for that. "Sorry, it's none of my business."

"It's okay," she said, waving her hand. "Jasper... I never really knew Jasper."

"You were in the same class." It sounded like an accusation.

"That doesn't mean anything," she said slowly, taking a step toward him. "Dinner last night was the longest we've ever talked."

It hit Cam then, crystal clear. Jealousy over that dinner was what had been bothering him all day. What had kept him awake the night before.

Feeling irritated even now, he wanted to pace. But she was standing so close. He could smell her perfume, a flowery scent that mixed with the aromas from the kitchen. Shouldn't go together, but to him, it was intoxicating.

"Look, Elle, just tell me, once and for all, do you have feelings for my brother?"

"No," she practically screamed. "And for the record, I would never go after someone who was taken."

"Great. I don't want you to do that."

"Then what do you want, Cam?"

"I want to kiss you."

"So kiss me."

She didn't even register her own words until his lips were on hers.

This was no ordinary kiss. Cam practically devoured her. Greedy, ravenous, moving over her lips so expertly that she forgot to be offended, appalled or even surprised. Instead, she fisted her hands in his shirt and pulled him closer.

Cam's response was a low guttural growl that made her feel insanely feminine, wanted, desired. When he yanked her up onto her toes, she went willingly.

They feasted on each other for minutes. Or maybe seconds. She wasn't sure. The only thing she could be sure of was that this was the most passionate kiss of her life.

When Cam pulled back, she wanted to protest. Instead, she looked into his eyes as they searched her face. His arms were wrapped around her tightly, possessively, as he kissed the tip of her nose, with such sweetness she almost cried. Then he took a step back and they stared at each other.

"Feel better?" she asked to break the silence.

"I definitely feel…something." He offered her a cocky, yet endearing, grin. His eyes raked over her from head to toe and back up again. Then he shoved his hands in his pockets. "Good night, Elle. See you tomorrow."

In a daze, Elle walked back into the kitchen. Holy crap. Cam Dumont could kiss. Pausing in the dim light, she pressed a finger to her swollen lips. They felt like they were on fire.

Funny how the last time she was in this house, all her thoughts of romance and passion were centered around Jasper. Now Cam dominated her mind.

Stopping suddenly, she clapped a hand to her mouth. *Oh, no. I can't like Cam.*

Dashing into her bedroom, she closed the door and leaned back against it. What was she doing? She couldn't kiss Cam. Not after liking his brother for most of her adolescent life. The entire town—not to mention that damn Bayside Blogger—would have a field day.

And that kind of attention was the last thing she wanted. Her dad would be beyond embarrassed.

There was only one thing to do. She would make sure she didn't kiss Cameron Dumont ever again.

Chapter Seven

Elle slammed the lid of the laptop down. "Damn Blogger," she muttered through clenched teeth.

How in the hell had she found out that Cam had been to her house the night before? After finishing the last gulp of coffee, Elle put her mug in the dishwasher.

"His truck," she said into the silence of the house. Her dad was still sleeping. Of course, anyone in town could have driven by and seen Cam's truck parked in front of her house. She grabbed her purse, sketch pad and notebook, and went on the porch to wait for Cam.

Glancing at the houses to the left and right, she wondered if one of her neighbors had been the little birdie who told on her. Maybe one of her neighbors was the Bayside Blogger.

Maybe they were watching now.

Paranoid. She needed to get a grip.

Cam's truck rounded the corner and pulled to a stop in front of the house. She rushed over and yanked the door open, even as Cam was getting out to open it for her.

She pointed to the road. "Drive."

His lips twitched. "Yes, ma'am."

The truck lurched into a U-turn and she scrunched down in her seat, trying to keep out of sight. Noticing her peeking over the edge of the window, Cam threw the truck into Park, turned toward her and placed his arm over the seat back. He leveled her with a questioning stare. "What gives?"

Scrunching down in her seat, she whispered, "I don't want her to see me."

"Who?" he asked, eyes darting around.

"The Bayside Blogger," Elle said through clenched teeth. "She's everywhere."

He chuckled. "Oh, is that all?"

"Cam, this is serious," she hissed. "Keep going and get off this block before more people see you on my street."

He obeyed, but she didn't miss his eye roll. "You're kidding, right?"

Once they'd cleared Bay View Road, she sat up straighter and smoothed her hair down. "The Bayside Blogger tweeted that you were at my house last night."

"So?"

Why were men so clueless? she wondered not for the first time in her life.

"I *was* at your house last night," he said.

"I know that. But now everyone else does, too."

He sneaked a glance at her before returning his attention to the road. "I don't see what the problem is." Flicking his signal on, he made a left turn toward the other side of the bay. "I had a good time last night."

The husky tone of his voice made her heart rate speed up as the memory of his lips on hers slammed into her mind. Even with his window down and the cool morning air filtering into the cab, she could feel her cheeks heating.

"This is traditionally where you say you also had a good time," he offered.

She wanted to. Even before that, she'd enjoyed watching him with her dad during dinner, and appreciated having a verbal sparring partner.

But there could be no more kissing. She'd decided that last night, and she needed to stick to her decision.

"I..." She didn't know how to finish that sentence. It didn't matter anyway, because Cam stopped the truck, gave her a long once-over and then announced that they'd arrived.

"Nice house," she commented, taking in the large brick home, circular driveway and tasteful landscaping.

"Tell me about it. I've done a lot of work on it since it was built two years ago."

They got out of the cab and walked toward the door together. "If it was only built two years ago, why have you done so much work? What could it possibly need?"

"Shoddy workmanship from the start," he said, knocking on the front door. "They hired an idiot contractor and the list of issues could wrap around Bayside three times over."

"But we're getting them all taken care of now." The statement was made by a pretty woman of about thirty years old, with a very pregnant belly, who appeared in the doorway.

Elle stepped into an impressive foyer with marble floors and a grand staircase leading up to the second level. A grand mirror on one wall enlarged the room, while framed photos and a few paintings on another wall gave it a homey feeling.

She turned to the woman, who was studying her closely. Cam made the introductions.

"Elle, this is Carson Rothchild. Carson, as I mentioned, Elle may be able to help with the mural you want for the nursery. She's an artist and just returned from Italy."

Carson's eyebrows shot up. "Italy? Really? That's impressive."

"Thanks," she replied. "I mostly worked in museums and galleries, but I do paint and may be able to help."

Seeming antsy, Cam switched from one foot to the other. Carson laughed. "Oh, go back, already. I know you're dying to see the shipment."

"It arrived okay?"

"Early this morning. Too early. You need to talk to your subcontractors about the importance of beauty sleep."

"Noted." Cam turned to Elle. "I'll just leave you guys to it then. Holler if you need me." With that, he walked back through the house like he owned it.

"New quartz countertops in the kitchen," Carson explained as she rubbed her belly.

"The things that excite some people," Elle said, rolling her eyes, and Carson laughed.

"Exactly." She steered them toward the staircase. "Come on up and I'll show you the nursery."

"When are you due?" Elle asked.

"Three months. Twins. Surprise," she said with a huge smile. They stopped outside a room. "This is it."

Elle walked in and struggled not to ooh and aah. The room was so sweet, with light colors on the walls, a plush carpet, two large bay windows and two cribs against one wall. "What an adorable room."

Carson walked a little circle before settling in a rocking chair. "I think so, too. We're having two girls, hence the pink-and-purple color scheme. But I'd really like that wall over there—" she pointed to it "—to have a floor-to-ceiling mural."

Elle examined the room and took into account the existing color palette, the decorations and toys already bought. Making a few notes, she also took the lighting into account.

"This is a really great space and there are so many fun directions you can take a mural. If you decide to go with me, I'd like to talk to you and get a feel for your interests, ideas and what kind of things you're thinking about already."

Leaning her head back on the rocking chair, Carson offered a wry smile. "If I hire you? Honey, you are hired."

Pleased, Elle felt extreme happiness at the idea of having a job. Even if it was only a short-time thing. "Thank you so much," she said.

"No, thank *you*. Once I set my mind on something, there's no going back. For whatever reason, I decided I had to have a mural. But you," she said, pointing at Elle, "are the first person to come in here and ask what I would like."

"Really?"

"Everyone else with the ability to do this kind of painting told me what I needed."

Elle laughed lightly. "Artists are crazy people."

"Crazy or not, I want you to do this."

"In that case, I'd like to take some measurements."

For the next two hours, the two of them chatted and got to know each other. Elle got the specs she needed and more. After talking to Carson she had a clear vision of what would work for the mural.

"When can you start?" Carson asked as she poured a cup of coffee for Elle. They'd moved down to the kitchen.

"I'm going to work on sketches tonight and should be ready to show them to you tomorrow. I can start as soon as you decide on the design you like best."

She passed sugar and a little white pitcher of cream to Elle. "You are a godsend." She took a sip of the tea she was having. "Now that all that work and art stuff is out of the way, I have to ask you something."

Smiling, Elle put her mug back on the table as she helped herself to one of the shortbread cookies Carson had set out. "Shoot."

"Well…I've been reading about you."

The bite of cookie she'd just taken sank like a ten-pound weight to the bottom of her stomach. "The Bayside Blogger?" she asked, already dreading the answer.

Nodding, Carson pushed her tea away. "I have to say that I'm curious. Are the things she's reporting true?"

Elle placed the other half of her cookie back on the plate. "No. Kind of. I guess." She let out a little half laugh as she tried to think what she should say.

Carson leaned forward. "I didn't mean to embarrass you."

She waved a hand. "You didn't. I embarrassed myself years ago."

"I'd rather have the truth from you than read it online."

Grateful for this refreshing viewpoint, Elle relaxed again. "Thank you. Some of the things are true. I did have a crush on Jasper in high school. And I did make a video declaring that love. And that video was played in front of the entire school at our senior prom. After prom I did fall into the bay, but that was an accident, trust me."

Saying all that out loud had her stomach churning and she shuddered a bit. She added, "But that was a long time ago. I don't have feelings for him anymore."

"Do you have them for anyone else? Come on, indulge a super pregnant woman."

"I haven't even thought about dating, to be honest."

Carson tilted her head, studied Elle. "I think someone has thought about dating you."

Curious, Elle met her eyes. "Really?"

"I saw the way Cam looked at you this morning."

Elle shook her head violently. "Oh, no, no, no. He didn't look at me any way."

Carson laughed. "That's not a bad thing. Cam's hot. And successful."

"He's great. But I really don't—"

"And when he's not being so broody, he's very sweet. You should think about it. Heck, if I was single, I would."

"You would what?" The man of the hour strolled into the room. Seeming comfortable in this house, he leaned over and snagged a cookie. As he bit into the shortbread, Elle's eyes were drawn to his lips. The lips that had been on hers less than twenty-four hours earlier.

Elle squirmed in her seat. "Nothing. We weren't talking about anything important."

The way her eyes darted between the two of them, Carson must have felt bad for Elle. "How are things in the bathroom?"

Cam shook his head and let out a long, low whistle. "That contractor really screwed you."

"If I had a nickel for every time he says that I'd be able to build this entire house from scratch again," she said to Elle.

"You're practically doing that already. How's it going here?" Cam asked.

"You finally brought me the right person for the job," Carson said.

Cam looked pleased. "That's good to hear." He turned to Elle. "I can run you home if you want to work on sketches. Or we can set up an area for you here."

"I think home would be good. My supplies are there." Honestly, she wanted to get away from Cam, because the more she was around him, the more she thought about that kiss, and the more she couldn't squash the thought that she wanted to do it again.

Carson walked them to the door. "I'll see you after lunch, Cam. Elle, so nice to meet you. I can't wait to see the designs you come up with."

As they walked to the truck, Cam reached for her arm, but Elle quickly evaded him. They could not touch. Not in public. Not anywhere.

Cam must have caught on to her mood because instead of opening her door, he kept his hand over the handle. "What gives?"

"Nothing gives. I'm anxious to get to work."

He studied her for another moment, his dark eyes roaming her face, searching for the cause of her behavior. Finally, he backed up, opened the door and watched her slide in. But instead of closing the door, he leaned in, planting one palm on the center console and the other on her headrest, boxing her in. With their faces a mere hairbreadth apart, he said, "Good. Because I would hope that kiss last night didn't scare you off."

Turned on beyond belief, Elle couldn't speak. So she shook her head instead.

"Great. Because I plan on doing it again soon."

The next week and a half was fairly uneventful. Unless Cam counted the fact that, due to working with a certain brunette artist every day, he tossed and turned at night and was losing sleep at an alarming rate.

Elle was a hard worker. There was no denying that. If he let her, she'd put in even longer hours that he did. In fact, she would get so engrossed doing her drawing and painting that he'd taken to giving her a thirty-minute warning at the end of the day.

He headed upstairs now for that very reason. But when he reached the nursery, he stopped right outside.

Once again, Elle was in the zone. She was wearing what Cam had come to think of as her working outfit. Every day she showed up in an old pair of overalls with a different color T-shirt underneath and a matching bandanna keeping the hair off her face.

Today, she had a smudge of paint on her cheek, and Cam twitched with the urge to cross the room and wipe it away. While he was there, he could take her in his arms again.

A noise drew him out of his lustful thoughts. He realized she'd begun humming. He wondered if she was aware that when she was in her element like this she wore a contented smile.

Cam was fascinated by her. Every day he found himself standing in the doorway for longer periods of time, watching her. He couldn't help himself—she was just so damn appealing, the way she became entranced in her art. She'd use large, exaggerated strokes sometimes; the brush swishing across the canvas. Other times, like today, she'd work on more intricate details. Her eyes would narrow and she'd steady her hand as she added different colors to the mural.

In a move he'd come to love, she'd step back, tap the handle of her paintbrush to her pursed lips and study her work. Her head would tilt this way and that as she considered.

This was a different side of Elle. An amazing side. He wished the entire town could see what he got to witness every day.

A small, sweet sound escaped her lips. She was pleased with her work today. Cam backed up. Maybe he could let her have a little more time today. Just this once...

A week later, Cam was still feeling pretty frustrated.

The work on the house was slightly ahead of schedule. He'd also just won a bid he'd been working on for a couple months.

But it didn't take a genius to figure out his irritation was rooted in the hot artist currently housed on the second floor.

He'd meant what he'd said to her in the truck. He did plan on kissing her again. But so far, he'd given her some time and space.

Ah, hell. Maybe he was the one who'd needed the time and space.

Damn woman had gotten under his skin. And when was the last time that had happened? Maybe his first crush back when he'd been what? Thirteen? Fourteen?

Women didn't usually get to him. He led a simple life

filled with hard work, a cold beer at night and lazy Sundays. Women had a way of complicating even the most basic plans.

Then why was it that all he could do lately was think about Elle? Wonder what Elle was doing when she wasn't working on the mural?

"Hey, boss," Tom, one of the younger guys on his crew, yelled. "That Ellie Owens chick wants to see you."

At the sound of her name, he whacked his thumb with the hammer he was wielding. "Dammit," he shouted.

Tom chuckled. "Ouch. You know, I typically aim for the wood. Not my finger."

Cam flicked a different finger up at Tom's smart remark. Then he descended the ladder and went off in the direction of the nursery.

Once he got there, he saw that he wasn't the only one. Carson, along with some friends, her sister who was visiting and the fancy interior decorator she'd hired were all standing in the hallway outside the nursery. Cam noticed a big pink bow was tacked to either side of the door and Elle stood next to it with a nervous smile on her face.

"What's going on?" he asked in a gruff voice.

"Oh, good, Cam's here," Carson said, excitement in her voice. "We're all here now so we can finally see." She was practically dancing in a little circle.

"Careful," Cam said. "Those babies might make an early appearance."

The women all laughed, but Cam didn't see what was so funny. He was serious.

When she let out a delicate cough, all eyes focused on Elle. "If I may have everyone's attention…" she said. "I want to thank Carson for giving me this opportunity. The mural is finished and I really hope you like it. So without further ado…" She gestured to the door.

Cam watched as Carson removed the pink bow and

slowly entered the nursery. He didn't need to be inside the room to hear her gasp of pleasure.

When he finally did poke his head in, he saw that Carson's hand was over her mouth and her eyes were filled with tears. Elle was standing to the side, hand to her own mouth, chewing on a nail. The other women were also staring at the wall, huge smiles on their faces as a chorus of oohs and aahs and "how sweet" and "so precious" filled the room.

Cam took another step in and his eyes roamed over the mural. He wasn't about to cry and sigh like the women, but he was impressed as hell.

"Oh, Elle," Carson said, grabbing her hand. "It's…it's so beautiful. I can't believe it."

"You like it then?" she asked shyly.

"Oh, my God, of course. It's beyond my wildest expectations. I mean, I know I approved the design, but this is just…to see it in real life… I can't believe how wonderful it is." Carson turned to him. "What do you think, Cam?"

He walked closer and took in the wall, painted in soft pastels. It depicted stars in the sky and a slender moon overlooking a grassy meadow with a stream running through it. There were two cherubs playing among the trees, as fairies watched them from the branches. Somehow Elle had managed to add touches of some kind of glitter that made it seem like fairy dust was being sprinkled over the babies.

"It's stunning," Cam said, stepping back from the wall. His breath caught at the sight of Elle's huge smile. He loved when she smiled like that and wished she'd do it more often. "Great work, Elle."

"Great?" Carson said. "This goes way beyond *great*. I can't wait to show all of my friends." She pointed at Elle. "I'm telling you, you are going to have so many people clamoring for your artistic skills, you're never going to have time to sleep again. This is the most perfect, wonderful, amazing nursery ever."

"Speaking of needing an amazing nursery..." Carson's friend Polly spoke up.

All the other women started squealing and Cam jumped back. Looking from one to the other, he had no idea what he'd just missed.

"You're pregnant?" Carson said in a high-pitched voice. "Oh, my God."

Beaming, Polly rubbed her belly. "A boy," she said with a huge grin.

More screaming ensued and Cam took another step toward the door and sanity.

"Elle," Polly said. "I'd like to be your first referral. Would you please consider doing something like this in my nursery?" She gestured to the mural. "Would you be able to do something for a boy?"

Nodding emphatically, Elle stepped forward, and the women started talking a mile a minute as ideas about murals for boys flew around the room.

Cam backed out of the room quietly, although with the level of noise inside, they wouldn't have noticed him, anyway. He made his way downstairs with a big smile on his face. Elle did good work and he was thrilled he was able to help her.

At the same time, disappointment settled into the pit of his stomach. Her job completed, Elle wouldn't be in the same place as him anymore. He'd come to look forward to eating lunch together, taking coffee breaks and driving her home at the end of each day.

But now she would move on. He knew he should do the same. The problem was, he didn't know if he could.

Chapter Eight

I've been receiving a lot of mail, tweets and Facebook messages asking about Ellie Owens. Sadly, our gal has been hiding. Would I lie to all of you? Nope, not a chance. But who knows? Maybe she'll pop up at the Bayside Spring Festival today...

"Do you really, really want to go to this?"

At her dad's stoic expression, Elle relented. But not without a silent sigh.

"I go to the Bayside Spring Festival every year. Why would this year be any different?" he asked.

"But do you really need me to go, too?"

Elle had been back in Bayside for almost a month now. Since she'd finished the mural for Carson Rothchild last week, she'd been in talks to not only do a mural for Carson's friend Polly, but to paint and design the entire room. As much as she was looking forward to that, the actual work wouldn't take place for another month.

Since none of the work had begun yet, though, she'd mostly been hiding out. Except for meeting Riley for coffee a couple times. In the meantime, Elle had decided the best way to stay off the dreaded Bayside Blogger site was to hide out at her dad's house. Even though she'd told her father she'd been busy job hunting—which she had—she was mostly trying to not do anything worth talking about.

"You have to get out of this house," he said, reaching for his hat and jacket.

This time, she couldn't hold in the sigh.

He looked over at her. "I mean, I'm still sick. And weak," he added with a big frown.

She wasn't buying it. Elle knew when she was being taken. After all, her dad had been outside planting flowers earlier. And the other day, he'd been at an all-day poker game with his old friends from the force. Not to mention his coloring looked much better and he was starting to gain a little weight back.

No, her dad wasn't frail and incapable of driving himself into town for the annual festival. There would be a couple different bands, lots of food and some boat races. Nothing strenuous whatsoever. In fact, it even sounded fun.

While the town hosted lots of different events in the busy summer tourist season, this festival was only for residents. A sort of early kickoff to summer and farewell to winter party.

But with everyone in town in attendance, Elle's chances of drawing attention to herself grew exponentially. Although…there was one person she'd kind of like to see.

Hating to admit it, Elle missed Cam's company. It was interesting how a man of so few words could make her smile and feel at ease.

But even the thought of bumping into Cam didn't have her running to the car.

"Remember, I have cancer," her dad said.

"Somehow, I don't think I'll forget that," she replied with a resigned sigh. Knowing she'd lost the battle, she grabbed her jacket and took the keys her father offered.

Ten minutes later, Elle had dropped her dad off near the center of town and circled around until she found a parking spot. Instead of getting out of the car, she stayed put. Maybe she could hide out here for the entire festival. Would her dad really notice if she didn't load up on funnel cake and overly sweet lemonade?

Tilting the rearview mirror, she checked her makeup and hair. Completely normal. Then she glanced down at her clothes. She'd put on a pair of dark jeans and a light pink top. Nothing flashy to draw attention.

She was completely average.

Still, her fingers bent around the steering wheel and held on tight. Breathing in and out, she centered herself, quiet and calm permeating the car. Until a tap on the window almost made her jump out of her skin.

"Cam," she said, as she rolled the window down.

Leaning in close, he gave a wry smile. "You know, I thought it was a one-time thing, but now I see you really don't understand the basic concept of getting out of a parked car. I'm willing to offer a class."

She rolled her eyes, pulled the key from the ignition and got out. "Ha-ha, aren't you hysterical."

After she locked the door, she took her first good look at him. He wore a pair of old jeans and a fitted blue jersey with his flannel jacket over it, and she noticed he hadn't shaved today. The stubble did something to her. Made her breath catch as she imagined kissing him again, having that stubble rub against her cheeks.

His dark eyes were watching her, flicking over her face. How bad would it be to just go up on tiptoe and press her lips to his, only for a second?

"Cam…" she began. Elle moved toward him, not believing what she was about to do. What she'd wanted to do for the last couple days.

Then a horn sounded and a group of teenagers came running by, ruining the moment.

Was that look on his face disappointment? she wondered. She hoped so. It would mirror her own feelings.

At least the interruption forced her to remember that she was in public and she did not want to draw any attention to herself today. So she offered Cam a small smile and began to walk toward the festival.

"How are things going at the Rothchild house?" she asked.

"No complaints. We're finally nearing the end." He fell into step alongside her.

"What will you do after this project? Do you have something else lined up?"

He nodded. "There's always more. I've been working on something with my brother, actually. That will need some attention soon."

"I miss seeing Carson every day."

"She's planning some kind of baby party thing."

Elle chuckled. "That's called a baby shower, and I got my invitation."

"So you'll be going?"

She slid him an odd look. "Of course. She wants people to meet the artist who did the mural. Could mean more business for me."

"I was starting to think you've been hiding out."

Shocked that he would figure that out, she stumbled on a rock. Cam reached for her arm before she could topple over. At his touch, her breath hitched.

"You okay?" he asked, his deep voice husky and thick with emotion. He didn't let go of her arm. Instead, he used the leverage to pull her closer.

"Yeah," she said, eyes plastered on his mouth. On lips that were within reach.

"Elle?"

She jumped, then turned to see Riley hustling toward them.

"You decided to come, after all! I'm so happy you stopped hiding away in your house." Riley looked back and forth from her to Cam, then raised an eyebrow.

"I haven't been hiding. I've been job hunting and it's kept me busy."

"Uh-huh," Riley said with a smirk. Sliding her arm through Elle's, she steered her toward the festival, with Cam following. "You have got to tell me what's going on with you two," she murmured.

Elle felt the heat on her face and was happy that Cam was walking behind them at the moment. "Shh," she whispered.

Riley laughed. "Come on, both of you. There's a decent band playing already and Mr. Healey is making some really good shrimp quesadillas."

The three of them entered the festival, and Elle took in the event that covered the entire town square, along with the marina and the surrounding docks. Seemed like every local business was participating. Tents and tables were set up in front of the storefronts, displaying various clothing, jewelry, accessories and more. Elle couldn't wait to do a lap.

She noticed The Brewside was handing out small samples of coffee, drinks and baked goods. Most of the restaurants had followed suit, giving away their various specialties and offering coupons and discounts. The mixture of yummy smells was better than any welcome mat.

Bayside hadn't forgotten about the kids either. Elle saw the middle of the square was dedicated to games with prizes of stuffed animals and small toys.

The festival was packed and everyone appeared to be having an amazing time. Laughter carried on the breeze and the sound warmed her heart. She'd really missed this festival while she was away.

On the far end of the square, they'd set up a stage and Elle, Cam and Riley listened to the band for about twenty minutes. While Riley and Cam headed off to get food, Elle sneaked away to check on her dad. Once again she realized she had no reason to worry, when she saw him holding court with a bunch of his buddies, laughter and curse words flying as they no doubt relived tales from their days as cops.

Meeting back up with Riley, she took the quesadilla her friend offered and they found seats on a nearby wall that overlooked the marina, where they could listen to the band and people watch at the same time.

After they finished their food, which was delicious, Elle asked, "Where's Cam?" She realized asking the question had been a mistake when she saw Riley's eye light up.

"He ran into someone from work. Okay, spill," her friend said emphatically.

"What?" Elle asked.

Riley's eyes grew huge. "What? Oh, my God, are you seriously playing coy?"

Elle took a sip of lemonade and shrugged her shoulders.

"I'm going to call you Ellie, which I know you hate, until you tell me what is going on between you and Cam Dumont."

Sputtering on her drink, Elle put the glass down and met Riley's smug expression. "Nothing is going on. I ran into him when I was parking and we walked over together. That's all."

Shaking her head, Riley tsked. "I don't believe you, Ellie. There's been something between the two of you since you got back. I mean, the way he looks at you—"

"How does he look at me?" Elle asked too quickly.

"See? I knew it. Do you have a thing for Cam?"

Elle dodged the question. "For the foreseeable future I'm going to be settled here in Bayside. I just want to find some work and keep a low profile. You know what I mean?"

Riley looked thoughtful for a moment. "The Bayside

Blogger? You don't want her to know about your crush on Cam?"

"I don't want to be the object of her column. I just need some time to settle back in. I've been gone a long time and coming home... Well, it's been harder than I thought it would be."

Once again, her thoughts turned to the video she'd made in high school. Truth was, she hadn't even known she was being filmed.

But she did know how disappointed her dad had been. She'd never forget the expression on his face when she'd gotten home from the prom.

Not until she'd been much older did she find out the full truth. She'd known that her dad had wanted to run for county sheriff, and she'd always wondered why he hadn't won the election. After all, he had the best qualifications of anyone on the force. He'd started off in New York City, and he'd been in the military before that.

Then she did some digging and found an old article from the *Bayside Bugle*. There it was in black-and-white—an op-ed piece talking about Ted Owens and his lack of control of his child.

That article had helped Elle to get her priorities straight. It had also been a jarring reminder that her dad had sent her away. But that had been her own fault. She'd been taking Italian classes since high school and decided that going to Italy—and staying there—would help her dad even more. The farther she got from Bayside, the better off her dad would be. Without his daughter to humiliate him.

Shaking her head, she tuned back to Riley, who was watching her intently. Reaching over, her friend squeezed her hand. "Don't worry, Elle. Everything is going to work out. You'll see."

A big splash sounded and they both turned in the direction of the bay. "Are people jumping in? Seriously?"

Riley asked. "The temperature may be starting to warm up, but that water is still freezing."

"Don't remind me," Elle said, making her friend laugh.

Elle noticed a group of people gathering at the dock. The hairs on the back of her neck stood in high alert. "What's going on?"

"Probably just some teenagers being teenagers," Riley suggested.

Elle started walking toward the dock—the same one she'd fallen from not too long ago—with Riley close behind. But a bad feeling niggled at her, even as Cam started running toward her, a worried look on his face.

"Hey, Elle," he called. "Come this way."

He tried to reach for her arm to steer her away from the crowd, but she sidestepped him and kept going.

But as she approached the dock, her heart nearly stopped. A huge sign erected right where she'd gone over the railing declared Jump for Love.

"There she is!" someone shouted.

Everyone present turned in her direction. Mortified, she heard the familiar whispers start up, saw Bayside residents all pointing at her as she walked forward, even while Cam and Riley called her back.

But wanting the full picture, she went all the way up to the dock, amid the sneers and whistles.

"Here she is, our little Ellie Owens." This was said by a guy she recognized from high school, but whose name she couldn't remember. "Come on up here, Ellie."

She planted her feet and stayed right where she was. Unfazed, the announcer continued with his spiel. "Ellie Owens jumped overboard for the love of Jasper Dumont. You, too, can take a turn, for only ten dollars. All proceeds go to the high school drama club."

Embarrassed beyond belief, she watched with wide eyes as a couple younger guys handed over some cash, gave

Elle a salute and jumped into the freezing water. A roar rose from the crowd.

"That idiot," Riley said through clenched teeth. "I'll never write a good review of a high school play again."

Appreciating the loyalty, Elle shook her head. "Don't take this out on the kids. They don't deserve it."

"What they deserve is a better example." Cam pushed through the crowd and starting walking toward the guy. Elle noticed his fingers curl into fists and jumped forward.

"No, no, no. Please, Cam. Let it be."

The crowd turned its attention in their direction, and for the second time that day she felt her cheeks heat up. But she managed to pull Cam back. As she did, Elle spotted her dad at the side of the crowd, his face ashen.

"My dad. I have to go talk to him." But even as she started to make her way in that direction, she watched him shake his head and walk away with one of his friends.

She'd done it again. Humiliated her father.

That left only one thing to do. Head held high, she pushed her shoulders back and made her way up to the dock. She reached into her purse, pulled out a ten dollar bill and shoved it into the guy's hand.

His face changed quickly. Even as some of the people in the crowd gasped and others laughed, the guy hosting this "event" lost his smile and his eyes went wide. Guilt practically poured out of him, but that wasn't her concern.

She'd begun walking away when the guy called out to her. "Wait, you, um, want to jump in?"

Elle paused, but didn't look back. Instead, she said loud enough for him to hear, "I've already had my turn." And she didn't stop walking this time until she'd reached her car and driven away.

Chapter Nine

My, my, the annual spring festival certainly provided the gossip this year. If anyone thought they were going to get away with making fun of little Ellie Owens and her high school shenanigans again, they might want to think twice! This hometown heroine left us all speechless yesterday with her act of charity in the face of adversity. Looks like the joke's on you, Dan Chumsky, for trying to embarrass her.

Sitting in his truck later that evening, Cam watched Elle's house for any sign of life. What he really wanted to do was go beat the living crap out of that thoughtless moron Dan Chumsky. He'd been a jerk in high school and clearly, not much had changed since then.

Watching Elle's face as she'd realized she was being ridiculed was one of the most painful things Cam had experienced in a good long time. Making the situation even worse was how heartbreaking it had been to watch her seek out her dad—only to have Ted turn away.

What the hell had that been about? Cam tightened his fingers around the steering wheel. *Poor kid*, he thought. He'd had a feeling she'd been hiding out for the last couple weeks. Now he knew he'd been right.

Well, the hiding was over, he thought as he pushed away from the steering wheel. Flicking his seat belt buckle, he growled. Elle was a good person. So she'd made one bad decision in high school. Hadn't they all done things back then they regretted?

The night was quiet. But then he heard what sounded like a door opening and closing, and he decided to take a chance.

Walking around the small house, he saw her on the deck. "Elle, listen here," he said, taking a step onto the deck. Her head snapped to the side and he froze.

It didn't look like she'd been crying, but there was definitely hurt and pain on her face. Her lips were pinched together and frown lines surrounded her eyes.

"Ah, hell." He bounded across the small space.

"Cam, what are you—"

Cutting off her question, he grabbed her and pulled her to his chest. That damn floral scent of hers infiltrated his senses as he held her close. She stood stiff in his arms for a few moments, before finally softening and letting out a long sigh.

I'm sorry about what happened today, Elle. But he couldn't quite get the words out. Instead, he tightened his grip on her.

When she pulled away after a couple minutes, he felt the loss. His body ached to be near hers again. Elle walked to the railing, hopped up and sat on it, facing him.

He propped an elbow beside her.

There was a certain sadness in her eyes. Even in the dark, Cam couldn't miss it and he hated it. "Listen, Elle," he began.

She held up a hand. "Stop. I know what you're going to say." She jumped down and turned to face the water. "It wasn't my fault. That guy's a jerk. I shouldn't let it bother me. Blah, blah, blah."

Pretty darn close to what he was going to say. Except for the blah, blah, blah.

She turned those pretty green eyes on him. Why did

she have the ability to make him want to melt with a simple stare?

"Well?" she asked. "Wasn't that what you were going to say?"

He threw an arm over her, boxing her in against the railing. "Not even close." With that, he brought his mouth to hers, taking her lips roughly, selfishly.

As fast as the kiss happened, he stopped it, pulling back, hoping he hadn't crossed any lines. But meeting her now-hazy eyes, he realized that Elle had enjoyed it as much as he did. So he leaned back in and brushed his lips over hers once, twice, three times, as gently as he could. Framing her face in his hands, he took her lips softly this time with small, tender kisses.

Elle sighed and folded into him. His palms left her face to circle her as she ran her own hands up his back, over his shoulders, and finally, into his hair.

Again he pulled back. This time, she smiled shyly and then tugged him toward her. With a not-so-gentle nibble, she sucked his bottom lip into her mouth, a sensation that had him inhaling sharply out of sheer pleasure. Then she plunged her tongue inside his mouth, and he didn't have the brain cells left to understand what was going on. Only that he'd never had a kiss that felt this damn good.

Cam had no idea how long they stood there, making out on the deck, as the water gently lapped and the moon shone down on them. But when they finally looked up at each other, he saw that her lips were swollen, the skin around her mouth was reddened from his stubble and her eyes were glazed.

It made him want to yell out in triumph.

Instead, he ran a finger over the soft, silky skin of her cheek. She shivered.

"You're a man of your word," she said, her voice husky.

"Excuse me?"

"The second kiss you promised me. It was good."

"Damn good," he agreed, grinning at her like an idiot.

She watched him for a long moment. Then her smile faded and her eyes cleared up. "But we can't keep doing that."

"Why the hell not?" he demanded.

Trying to push away from him, she furrowed her brow when she realized he was holding her tight, with no plans to let go. "Because," she continued. "I didn't come home for a love affair. And I certainly didn't return so I could keep humiliating myself."

"Does kissing me humiliate you?"

She winced. "No, I didn't mean that."

"Why'd you come home then?" he asked simply.

"For my dad. I should have been here the day after he was diagnosed. Would have been if he'd told me," she stated. "Cam, I embarrassed him today."

"You think kissing me would embarrass Ted?"

"That's not what I mean." She swung her head back and forth. "I can't keep kissing the brother of the guy I was in love with in high school. People will—"

"Talk," he finished for her. "They'll always talk. They'll always gossip. So what? Your business is *your* business. Who cares what these people think?"

She laughed at that and Cam enjoyed seeing her face light up.

"You need to get away for a day," he blurted. She tilted her head and he figured why stop now. "I have a cabin, about an hour from here. It's nothing special, but going there always helps me clear my mind. Tomorrow's Sunday, and I thought I might go fishing. Why don't you bring your notebook and paints and stuff? Keep me company." Had he really just gone on and on like a bumbling preteen?

Elle kept her mouth closed and didn't say a word. He could see the wheels of her brain turning. Clearly, she was trying to figure out all the reasons—probably valid reasons—why she shouldn't go with him.

Then, she surprised him.

"What time should I be ready?"

The next morning, Cam practically jumped out of bed. Truth be told, he hadn't planned on going to the cabin today, and he certainly hadn't planned on inviting Elle.

He'd bought and remodeled the cabin three years ago, and tried to get up there as often as he could. He didn't need to be anyone special there. He didn't need to be a Dumont. He could relax and forget about the world, while wearing a pair of ratty sweats and not combing his hair.

Which was why it didn't make any sense that Cam showered, slapped on some aftershave, ran a comb through his hair and picked out a pair of recently washed jeans and a black shirt.

"Where you going so early?"

He spun around at the sound of his brother's voice. Jasper strolled over from his car to where Cam was hoisting his fishing equipment into the bed of the truck.

"Thought I'd get in some fishing today," he explained, not quite meeting his brother's eye.

"Want some company?"

Something in Jasper's voice sounded off. He stood before Cam wearing clothes that were more than likely the same from last night.

"Been home yet?" Cam asked.

"Nah. I was at Mindy's."

Hope rose in Cam's chest. If Jasper spent the night with Mindy, that meant they were still together, which implied Jasper wasn't interested in Elle and therefore Cam wouldn't have to back off.

He shook his head and threw a six-pack of beer in the back. "Things are good between the two of you then?"

Jasper looked to the side.

"Jasp?" he prompted. Leaning against the bed of the truck, he waited. When it became clear Jasper wasn't going to say anything more, Cam demanded. "What the hell's going on?"

His brother shrugged. "Got into it with Dad last night. Couldn't sleep."

Cam jutted his chin forward in question.

"Same old," Jasper offered as explanation. "I had an idea—a good idea—and Dad rejected it. Immediately. Without even hearing me out." He began pacing back and forth in the driveway. "How am I supposed to accomplish anything if he won't loosen the reins?"

Cam knew that Jasper's gripe wasn't a one-time thing. Butting heads with their parents was becoming a daily occurrence. And that was all Cam's fault. If Jasper hadn't done him the favor of stepping into his shoes so Cam could go off and start his own company, his little brother wouldn't be so damn miserable all the time.

"Listen, Jasp…" Cam ran a hand over his face while he tried to figure out what to say. "I'm sorry. If you want to ditch this job, you know you can always come work for me."

Jasper's lips twitched. "Work for you? As what, exactly?"

"Well," Cam said. Then his own lips broke into a grin. Jasper didn't exactly know how to use his hands, he didn't like to get dirty and he pretty much hated everything about construction except the final product. "I'd make up something for you." And then he could stop feeling guilty over his brother.

Jasper's eyes softened. "I know you would. But I think all those degrees I've acquired might help me in securing a position somewhere less…rustic." He stuffed his hands in his pockets. "So, I repeat. Want any company?"

Clearly, this fight had been rougher than usual, because in the three years Cam had owned the cabin, Jasper had been there maybe twice. Jasper claimed he wasn't an "outdoor kind of guy" even though the cabin boasted every amenity Cam had in his regular house.

"Actually..." Cam began. Damn, he felt like such a jerk. His brother was obviously hurting, but what Cam really wanted was to spend the day with Elle. Alone.

"It's okay," Jasper blurted out, saving him from making a tough decision. "You know I don't really like that woodsman life."

"I have a huge plasma TV, cable, a hot tub and a wine fridge for my 'woodsman life.'"

"Whatever. There are trees and bunnies and stuff up there."

Cam chuckled, silently relieved. Though, man, his brother looked rough today. "But seriously, everything good with Mindy?"

Jasper looked away again. Then he quickly launched into it. "She's mostly fine. Still kind of weirded out about me having dinner with Elle. Doesn't help matters that Elle is so freaking hot."

In the middle of hoisting a bin of fishing supplies, Cam fumbled and the box landed with a loud crash in his truck.

"Careful, dude," Jasper said. "Anyway, I heard about what happened to Elle at the festival yesterday. That's messed up."

"It was definitely messed up."

"She okay?"

"I think she's going to be fine."

"Maybe I'll stop by her house today."

"No," Cam blurted out, before silently cursing himself. Jasper's head snapped up. "I mean, I think you showing up at her house after what happened yesterday would probably embarrass her."

"Makes sense." Jasper tucked his tongue in his cheek and handed Cam a small bag he'd put some essentials in. Cam tossed it in the truck. "You're acting weird, Cam."

He didn't know why he didn't come clean and tell his brother about Elle, only that he wanted to keep that little secret to himself. "Didn't sleep well myself. Anyway, I should be getting on the road."

Jasper studied him for a long time. So long that Cam had to suppress the urge to shuffle his feet and duck his head.

"Sure." Jasper slapped a hand on the truck and started walking back to his car. "Whatever you say." He got in his vehicle, clearly not buying any of it. He rolled down the window and shot Cam an unreadable look. "Well, have a good time. By yourself." He threw the car in Drive, but didn't pull away from the curb.

"Will do," Cam answered.

"Oh, and Cam?"

"Yeah?"

"Tell Elle I said hi." With that, Jasper grinned, peeled out and sped around the corner.

Cam stood at the bottom of the driveway, shaking his head. His brother could be right. Their parents truly didn't give Jasper enough credit. Apparently, Cam didn't, either.

Chapter Ten

A little over an hour later, Cam put the truck in Park and climbed out. After helping Elle from the vehicle, he grabbed a couple grocery bags and walked up to the front door. He found the right key on his key ring and let them inside.

Elle's intake of breath gave him a feeling of pride.

Shoving past him, she looked around the cabin, soaking in every detail, from the pictures on the walls to every piece of furniture. She made her way to the living room, studying everything as if there would be a quiz on it later.

For his part, Cam stayed in the entryway, trying to acclimate to seeing her in his space. He'd never brought a woman here before. Would the cabin retain the scent of her delicious floral perfume after she left? Would he think about her now every time he crossed the threshold?

"Cam, this is way beyond what I thought it would be."

He put the bags down. "What'd you think it would be like?"

"I don't know." She spun in a circle. "A one-room serial-killer type of place with an outhouse and no running water, maybe." She walked farther into the cabin as he chuckled. "Clearly, I'm an idiot. This is stunning."

So was she, and he liked the way she was reverently touching the wooden panels along the wall.

He gestured at the open concept, complete with vaulted ceilings, old wooden beams and skylights. "Kitchen is right there. This is the living area. Three bedrooms upstairs."

He tapped on a door around the corner from the living room. "This is a powder room. Two full baths upstairs."

"This is great. And look at these views." She wandered to the wall of windows that overlooked the large deck. Beyond it were trees, with mountains in the distance. Plus the lake below, with his own personal dock extending into it.

"Hot tub is out there, and access down to the water." He felt shy all of a sudden. "Gonna get this stuff inside. I brought some food for lunch and dinner. Want to come down to the dock while I fish?"

She nodded, but kept running around the house, looking at each room and space. Stopping at every window, she would glance outside, let out an appreciative sound and move on to the next. It was like watching a little kid in a toy store.

"It's official," she announced, when she returned from exploring the upstairs. "I'm in love with this place. I don't know why you don't just live here permanently."

Cam threw the last item from the cooler into the fridge. "Believe me, it's tempting. But since the majority of my work is in, or near, Bayside, the commute wouldn't be fun. It is peaceful, though." With a proud glance around the room, he took a moment to admire his own handiwork. His eyes flicked up to find Elle watching him with a smile.

Embarrassed, he reached for the mini cooler he kept at the cabin. "So, sandwiches okay for fishing?"

Her eyes lit up. Cam would even go so far as to say they sparkled. If he used a word like *sparkle*, that is, which he clearly did not.

"Cam, you have a lot to be proud of." She moved to the door that led out to the deck. With her hand on the knob, she stopped. "And sandwiches are fine."

Two hours later, they were seated at the end of the dock. Sandwiches had been consumed, Cam had drunk a beer, while Elle had stuck to diet soda. He had already caught one fish and was feeling pretty good about his chances for more.

Next to him, perched on a wooden bench he'd built as part of the dock, Elle was scribbling away on her large drawing pad. She'd look up occasionally, or violently flip a page, but for the most part, she'd been quiet and keeping to herself.

Good thing he didn't need to concentrate after his line was in the water, though. While Elle sat silently, he kept stealing glances at her. She looked pretty in the early-afternoon light. The warm spring sun beat down on her, illuminating her shiny hair and smooth skin. She looked at home here. She was wearing a dark purple top with a plaid blouse over it and a pair of jeans. Cam couldn't help but notice how those jeans fitted her just right as they'd walked from the cabin down to the lake. Her hair was tied back in some kind of intricate braid and he liked how it was away from her face. He really liked her face.

"What are you thinking?" Elle asked. Her voice startled him from his very nonmasculine train of thoughts.

Obviously, he wouldn't let her know what he'd really been considering, so he improvised by reaching over and tapping her sketch pad. "I enjoy watching you work and I'm wondering what is keeping you so preoccupied."

"Do you want to see?"

She bit her lip for a split second. But it was enough to let Cam know that showing her work made her nervous. And also highlighted that oh-so-tempting mouth.

"I'd like that very much."

Taking a moment, she looked down at the page before handing her pad over to him.

Cam shifted in his seat as his eyes raked over the drawing. It was damn good. He already knew she had a natural flair for art after the mural she'd done. But this was different. It was great, too, but less busy, with simple, clean lines.

"You know what I find interesting?" he asked. "You wanted to get away from Bayside and yet you're drawing it." He nodded at the rendition she'd done of the town square.

A slight blush reddened her cheeks. Sitting back, she studied her drawing as Cam handed it back. "Huh. I hadn't realized," she said, more to herself than him.

Cam propped his legs on the cooler. "What's your deal with Bayside, anyway? Why all the angst?"

Huffing out a breath, she offered him a look that should have made him feel like an idiot. "Oh, I don't know. Maybe because I massively embarrassed myself and my dad by making a drunken video about your brother?"

"Oh, is that all," he teased. "I hold firm that you give way too much credence to the opinions of our beloved townsfolk."

"Easy for you to say from way over there. They won't let me forget about it."

"You don't have to acknowledge it. You know," he began, deciding to switch tactics, "I kind of liked that you declared your love for Jasp. No, really," he said, in response to her rolling eyes. "You were passionate and there's nothing wrong with being vocal about your passions. Although, to be honest, I never did understand what you saw in him back then."

Her mouth fell open. "Cameron Dumont, he's your brother."

"So the doctors claim. But I have my own suspicions."
She smiled.

He shifted in his seat. "If I remember correctly, you were a really good student. Bright, smart, but shy, too."

She nodded. "Unlike most teenagers, I liked learning.

I was top of my class." Her eyes lost focus. "Or I was supposed to be."

"The video?" he asked.

"The video," she confirmed with a sigh. "And you're right. I was shy, too."

He sat back, studied her. "I've never understood that, either. You had a lot going for you."

She shrugged and then took a sip of her soda. "I think part of it is just how I am. But the other part had to do with losing my mom so young. My dad was great. He did an amazing job, but…"

"I get it. Must have been tough on both of you. Alpha-male cop like your dad trying to raise a little girl."

"Exactly. I've never really craved attention. I'm content to sit on the sidelines and watch."

"So here's my question."

"Ah, we finally get to the question." She tilted her head toward him.

"How does the smart, shy, never-step-a-toe-out-of-line girl end up getting wasted and making a video about my brother?"

"It was a mistake."

Mulling that over, he knew there was more to the story. "An out-of-character mistake. I never bought it. What really happened back then?"

She fidgeted on the bench. "I had been drinking that night," she said in a soft voice. "Only I didn't know it."

Now they were getting to the truth of the matter. And a truth that Cam had suspected for a long time. "Someone spiked your drink?"

"Two someones. I don't know if you remember them, but there were these girls in my class, Samantha and Parker."

Cam dug back and could vaguely picture them, sort of remembered their names. "The popular girls?"

"Understatement of the year. The thing is, I knew who they were, the kind of girls they were. The night before senior prom, they invited me for a sleepover. The same girls who had never spoken to me before. You'd think I would have figured it out."

She walked to the edge of the dock, crossed her arms in front of her, then turned back to face him. "Why would two of the most popular girls in our class invite a person they'd ignored since elementary school to a sleepover at the end of senior year?" He shrugged. "They'd found out about my feelings for Jasper."

She stepped closer, but didn't sit down. "They said we were drinking lemonade. It tasted like lemonade, only I remember feeling woozy and loose almost immediately. And then they told me they'd always wanted to be friends with me, but were afraid they weren't smart enough. I was so touched." She shook her head. "Stupid."

Cam really started feeling for her. "You were young. Naive."

"Sheltered. Don't tell my dad I said that." She offered a small smile. "After the enhanced lemonade, we started talking about boys. They went right to Jasper."

"How did they know about your crush on my brother?"

"They found my journal. I'd left it in the art room one day. God, Cam, that journal was so embarrassing. It was filled with all of my adolescent feelings for your brother. With illustrations and really bad poetry."

"So they found the journal, read it, used it against you, got you drunk and then made a video of you?"

Sitting back down, she concentrated on her old sneakers. "That pretty much sums it up. When they played it at prom, I just stood there, shocked. I'll never forget that feeling in my stomach. It was so awful. Everyone laughing, staring, pointing."

She shivered, even though it wasn't cold with the late

afternoon sun beating down on the dock. "In the video, I was wearing this really oversize shirt I used to sleep in. It had slipped off my shoulder and exposed my bra. And maybe a little more than that." She covered her face with her hands. Then she peeked through her fingers. "The principal thought I did it on purpose."

Cam stood abruptly and Elle's head snapped up, her hands falling to her lap. "Speaking of Principal Baker, why the hell didn't he go after those girls?"

A red blush tinted her cheeks. "Because I never told on them."

"Why not?" He sat next to her and grabbed her hands. "What they did was *not* okay. They got you drunk, stole your property, embarrassed you. In fact, the whole thing could have been a lot worse."

She tried to pull her hands from his, but Cam held on tight. He wanted to shake her. Why didn't she see how wrong this was? All these years the entire town had thought she'd done this inappropriate little thing. But in reality, she'd been the victim of two very mean bullies.

Finally, she freed her hands and stood. "Despite it all, they were still the popular girls. And I wanted to impress them. I was very inexperienced with…everything."

"You didn't get to be valedictorian." He rose now, as well.

"That doesn't matter. I had already been accepted into college."

"It does matter, Elle." He grabbed her upper arms. "It matters."

As her lips turned up in a sad smile, she met his eyes. "When my dad came to pick me up that night, I realized not being valedictorian didn't mean anything. Having the entire school laugh in my face wasn't a big deal. Because the completely silent ride home in our car gave me the time to think about it. Really think about it. The look on my dad's face was the worst thing in the entire world. That's what mattered."

She took a deep breath. "My dad couldn't get me packed up fast enough. He enrolled me in a presemester program that summer. Dropped me off in June. Because I'd disappointed him. That's the worst part of the story. The only person who ever loved me."

Cam's heart hurt for her. Did she really believe that? Ted Owens was a lot of things, but disappointed in his only child was not one of them.

"Being back here is so hard. I've missed the place. Before that incident, I loved Bayside. I felt safe here, you know? How ironic." She waited a beat. "When I was in Italy, I really missed my dad. But the stares and the whispers and that damn blog… Well, it's just difficult."

Cam wasn't good with words. Never had been. So he used action instead, and wrapped her in his arms.

When she pulled back, Elle framed his face with her hands. "Thanks for listening. It's really nice to have a friend."

His libido, nearly ready to charge out of the gate just being so close to her, feeling her body in his embrace, slammed on the brakes at the *f* word. His eyebrow shot up. "Is that what we are, Elle? Friends?"

She pressed her lips to his, softly at first. But then she poured herself into the kiss and Cam reaped the benefits of her passion.

"Special friends," she whispered against his mouth.

Taking in her swollen lips and hazy eyes, he had to agree. "*Special* sounds pretty damn good."

Chapter Eleven

Later that afternoon, Cam carried three fish back to the cabin. Elle wasn't usually into fish guts, but she had to admit it was kind of swoony to watch a super hot, totally alpha male clean and gut food that he'd caught with his own two hands. If only he'd done it shirtless...

Elle bit her lip at the thought and got to work herself while Cam grilled the fish out on the back deck. She set the table and threw together a salad with ingredients he had brought from home. She found premade potato salad and a bottle of red wine in the kitchen, as well.

When Cam returned with the cooked fish, she was sipping a glass. Nodding to the counter, she said, "I poured you some."

Now that she looked around at the food he'd brought and saw all the effort he put into their one-day trip, she realized that Cam Dumont was a really considerate guy. Even as she thought it, he pulled out a chair for her to sit down. Then he grabbed two candles, placed them in the center of the table and lit them. When he turned the overhead light low, the ambience became dreamy and romantic, and a little flutter started in her belly.

Despite the setting, they got through dinner with the conversation flowing smoothly from one topic to another. The fish was beyond delicious. But more than feeling satisfied over the food, she felt calm after the entire day. Elle hadn't realized how tightly wound she'd been.

"So," she said. She folded her napkin and placed it on the table. "Tell me about your job."

"Not much to tell."

She shook her head. "Of course there's something to tell. Besides, I've been yammering on and on about myself all day long." She pointed at him. "Your turn."

"You want to hear about my latest construction bid?"

He truly looked puzzled and it made her giggle. "No, silly, I want to hear about what made you start the company. I was surprised you weren't working for your parents."

"So were they."

His mouth was set in a grim line and his eyes had narrowed.

She stood and held out a hand. After a moment, he took it and let her lead him to the couch. "Tell me about it," she said softly, as she settled back into the comfy plaid cushions.

Cam sat, but wasn't able to get comfortable. "Are you cold? Want me to start a fire?" he asked, pointing at the fireplace.

She cocked an eyebrow. "Cameron Dumont, stop stalling. I'm not a reporter. I'm your special friend, remember?"

His grin came fast. "That's what we should get back to talking about. Actually, maybe not talk…"

"Cameron."

"Fine. I started my company about five years ago." He leaned back against the cushions. "I love construction. Love working with my hands, building things from the bottom up. I like the hours. I like working outdoors.

"I used to go to construction sites with my dad back in the day. It was my favorite thing to do with him. Only, he didn't realize how much it drew me… I started working some construction in the summers, on weekends."

"He thought you were studying the business, I bet," she

said, as Cam took a long gulp from a bottle of water. "Did you ever tell him how much you liked it?"

"Nope. Probably would have been easier on all of us if I had." He tilted the bottle to his lips again and this time finished the whole thing. "My entire life I was being groomed to take over the family business. Every party, every holiday, every bit of time I spent with my parents was about the damn business.

"Somewhere along the line, I came to a realization. I didn't want to be part of it, at least not in the traditional way. I wanted to start a construction department, head it up. I wanted it to be part of Dumont Industries. And about five and a half years ago, after endless hours of hating my job and being bored beyond belief sitting behind a desk in a suit and tie, I presented my idea to my parents."

"I didn't realize your company was tied to Dumont Incorporated," she said.

"It's not."

He said this with zero inflection or emotion, and Elle met his eyes. She could see the pain there. She would have to be blind to miss it.

"Putting it together now?" he asked. A muscle in his jaw ticked. "They acted like I'd deserted them. All I wanted was to do something that would make me happy."

Cam got up and walked to the mantel, propped an arm on it and stared into the unlit fireplace. "That was a rough time. We fought constantly. It was worse with my dad. He really didn't understand." He turned back to face her. "Acted like I was throwing my life away."

"You wanted to start a business. Most parents would be beyond thrilled if their kid showed that kind of initiative. I mean, I get that they were upset. But it seems kind of old-fashioned for them to be so upset about you not wanting to take over the company. You, the oldest child, shunning his birthright and all that."

"I agree. But I get where they were coming from, too. My dad and my granddad worked really hard to get that company where it is today. They have a lot of pride about it."

"But Jasper stepped up."

Cam remained quiet.

"Wasn't that a good thing?" she prodded.

He returned to sit next to her on the couch. "Jasper only stepped up to help me. I'm his big brother and I always tried to protect him, shield him from stuff. But one night we went out to a bar. I had one too many drinks and just let go and told him everything that was on my mind. The next morning he offered to take my place. My parents were less than thrilled. Jasper had done really well in school, but he hadn't been groomed the way I had. He'd never worked for the company. He always found internships and jobs with other real estate companies. Drove my dad nuts."

"So what happened? Because I already know that you did form your company and Jasper does work for your parents. What made them change their minds?"

"Lack of options, I suppose. They cut me off. I mean, I still have my inheritance, but they wouldn't help with my business at all. That's fine with me, actually. I'd been saving for a long time and was able to get a great loan."

His eyes shone with pride and it made her smile. Elle could only hope she would find some kind of work that made her feel the same sense of satisfaction.

"Every day I'm thankful for what I have and what I built. But even as I take a moment to enjoy it, I'm reminded that my little brother is across town fighting with my parents. They're all miserable and it's all because I wanted to work with my hands."

She leaned close and rapped him on the chest. "Passion."

"Huh?"

"Earlier, out on the dock, you said there's nothing wrong with being passionate."

"Yeah, so?"

"You were—you are—passionate about your company. I imagine you would have to be passionate to start a business from the ground up."

He blew out a long breath of frustration. "It hasn't been the same. Since I stopped working for my parents, it hasn't been the same between us."

"Of course it hasn't." His gaze flicked up to meet hers and she almost laughed at his perplexed expression. "Things change, Cam. Relationships evolve. That's how life is. Your relationship may have transformed no matter what you'd chosen to do." She rubbed a hand over his arm. "Have you ever talked to them about how you feel?"

The look he gave her made Elle want to laugh in his face. She may as well have asked him to eat mud-covered liver.

"You want me to talk about my feelings?" he asked, with zero emotion in his voice.

"It's not about what I want. It's about what you need. And from everything you've told me, it sounds like you need to talk with your folks."

"Maybe," he grumbled.

She decided to let it go for now. He'd probably had enough talking for a lifetime, although Elle was glad she knew the whole story now. But if she had to guess, his parents probably had no idea he felt this way. Not to mention his brother. When she'd had dinner with Jasper a few weeks back, he'd all but admitted his own angsty situation. Did Cam know anything about how Jasper felt? It probably wasn't her place to interfere.

"Hey, your turn." His gruff voice brought her back to reality. "What are you thinking?"

"Well," she began, studying him from her end of the

couch. "I was thinking that if you'd told me back in high school that I would be sitting here with Cameron Dumont, I would have thought you were crazy."

This statement appeared to shock him. "Really? Why?"

"Because you were Cam Dumont, older guy with a beard."

"I wasn't that much older. Just four years."

"Four years is a lot in high school," she said.

He scooted closer. "How about now?"

Glancing at him, she cocked her head. "No, four years seems great right about now."

She emphasized her statement by closing the remaining distance between them and planting her lips against his.

Cam met Elle's mouth with enthusiasm. Everything about today had been awesome. Normally, he considered this cabin his sanctuary. But the funny thing about Elle was that she seemed to fit right in and take everything in stride.

She'd sat with him while he fished, helped get dinner together and had been pleasant company. He'd honestly enjoyed his time with her. Even the talking part. Still, he couldn't deny that kissing her had been in the forefront of his mind the entire day.

Now it was happening. She inched closer, pressing her body against his. A guttural growl escaped his lips at the feel of her, soft and smooth and sexy as hell. His arms came around her protectively as he pushed his tongue into her mouth.

Somewhere in the back of his mind a voice was telling him to slow down or stop altogether. But that voice was dim to begin with and Cam had zero trouble completely dousing the sound.

Instead, he pulled her even closer as he pressed his lips against her neck. She made a little sound that he enjoyed, so he continued to run his mouth up and down the column of her neck as she grabbed his shirt, bunching it between her fingers.

She smelled so freaking good. As he made his way up to nip right behind her ear, he got a whiff of that floral scent again and it drove him crazy. He knew his breathing had become erratic and his pulse was off the charts, but he tried to stay in control.

Then she did something that surprised the hell out of him. Without warning, she leaned back, offered up a coy smile and then pushed him back against the pillows.

"There," she said and straddled him.

"Happy, are you?"

"Shut up and put your mouth on me again." But she didn't wait around, instead plastering her lips against his as her hands became very busy wiggling their way under his shirt.

As her silky fingertips glided over his skin and entwined in the hair on his chest, he became helpless to do anything remotely suave. Elle was in total control, and hell if that didn't turn him on even more.

Of course, she noticed. How could she not, when her jean-clad bottom was sitting right on top of that need? On cue, she began circling her hips against his erection while she continued to assault his lips. Her hands stayed busy, too. When they reached the top of his pants, he let out a whoosh of breath. Her fingers running over that very sensitive spot cleared every thought out of his mind.

He clamped his hands on her hips, dug his fingers in and flipped her onto her back. Letting out a little laugh, she drew her bottom lip into her mouth, and Cam knew for certain right then and there that she was going to be the death of him.

And what a great way to go.

"Gonna stare at me all night?"

"No, ma'am," he growled in a gruff voice. She reached

for the hem of his shirt and yanked it up and over his head. Then he covered her body with his, loving the way they fit together. In fact, he was so happy that he heard that ringing again. Only this time Elle stopped kissing him.

Their confused eyes met, and after a brief moment, they both smiled.

"My phone," she said, her voice breathy and light. Her cheeks flushed with color. "Ignore it."

"You got it." And he happily returned to running his hands from her waist up her sides and circling her breasts. She had the best body and he wanted to explore every inch of it. He didn't care if...

Ring, ring.

Okay, so he would destroy her phone and then explore every inch of her.

Ring, ring.

She murmured against his lips, the sound conveying pleasure, need and want. He understood the feeling. He unbuttoned her blouse and then hastily pushed it off her, along with her T-shirt. All Cam wanted at the moment was to feel her skin against his.

But first he had to take a second to soak her in. Her breasts were pushed up against a lacy pink bra, inviting and sexy as hell. He leaned down to get a better taste.

Ring, ring.

While he was enjoying running kisses along the enticing curve of her breasts, as her breath came out in short little spurts, that damn voice that he'd extinguished earlier roared back to life. Her phone had gone off multiple times. Something nagged at him to sit up and pay attention.

"Hey," she protested, as he pushed himself up to his knees.

"Your phone." His voice came out in a croak and he had to take a second to steady his racing heartbeat. He'd had more game as a pimply high school kid.

But as he got some distance from her, he realized why they had to break apart. Her dad might need her. Who else would call multiple times?

"Your dad," he said.

"Is definitely not someone I want to think about while we're shirtless together." But then her playful smile faded and she must have realized the same thing. "Where's my phone?" she asked, a worried expression on her face as she scooched up into a sitting position.

"Here," he said, finding it under her discarded shirt.

Her eyebrows drew together and her lips pursed as she studied the screen. "I don't know this number, but it's a Bayside area code."

Pressing a couple buttons and then holding the phone to her ear, she listened until her face fell and her eyes widened.

"What's wrong?"

She put the phone down even as her bottom lip began to tremble. "It's my dad. He's in the hospital."

Chapter Twelve

Elle stood in the sterile hallway of Bayside Memorial Hospital, unmoving and unblinking. That distinctive smell of antiseptic and bleach infiltrated her nose as a doctor's name echoed over the loudspeaker.

Finally, she shook her head and tried to concentrate on the doctor standing in front of her. Wearing his white coat, a stethoscope slung around his neck, he scanned the clipboard in his hands.

Elle took a deep breath. "So you're telling me that nothing is wrong with my dad?" Still in a state of shock and disbelief, she ran her hands through her hair.

Again the doctor searched his chart, checked something off with his pen and then looked up. "We've run a series of tests since his friends brought him in. Everything's coming up negative—which is good in this case," he quickly added.

"But he collapsed. His friends said he was out of breath." She clamped down on the urge to scream. She and Cam had broken all speed records getting back to Bayside, only to find her dad lounging in his hospital bed with a bowl of pudding in one hand and the remote to the wall-mounted television in the other.

Elle leaned forward and whispered, "My dad has cancer."

To his credit, the doctor offered a genuine smile. "Since I happen to be his oncologist, I am aware of that." Reaching in his pocket, he produced a business card. "Here is all of my information. Your father's one of my favorite patients. He's also one of my orneriest."

"Thank you. And you're sure that his collapse had nothing to do with the cancer...? What?" she asked, seeing the grin that appeared on the doctor's face.

"You should talk to your dad. I think you'll get a better picture of what really happened today. In the meantime, he's going to be just fine. We'll keep him overnight and run a couple more tests. More than likely he'll be released first thing tomorrow morning."

"Thank you." As the doctor walked away, Elle narrowed her eyes and tried to process the events of the day. Even though she was still worried about her father's sudden collapse, now that she could see that he was okay her adrenaline was falling and exhaustion was taking over.

She pressed her shoulders back and pushed through the door to his room.

"Hey, sweetie," he said. "Doc said I have to stay overnight. At least the game's on." He pointed the remote at the TV.

"Right," Elle said wearily. "Do you want me to stay here with you tonight?"

"Of course not. All I'm going to be doing is sleeping. And hopefully eating more pudding."

She rolled her eyes. "Are you sure? Because I don't mind."

"No, I'll be just fine."

"Speaking of being fine, the doctor said your collapse had nothing to do with the cancer." When he didn't say anything, Elle pushed. "What do you think it had to do with?" Still nothing. She snatched the remote from his hand and turned off the game.

"Hey!"

"What did you do today?"

"Nothing."

She cocked an eyebrow and crossed her arms over her chest.

"Honestly, sweetheart. I just hung out with the guys. A typical Sunday."

Not buying it, she began tapping her foot in an irritated rhythm.

"Okay, we might've overdone it a little bit."

"Overdone it? What exactly were you doing with your friends?"

"Don't get upset. There's this thing I've always wanted to do, and Herb thought it would be fun. He also went through a bout with cancer last year."

Uncrossing her arms, Elle pinned her dad with a stare. "What was the thing?"

"Just this little activity that's been on my bucket list."

"Care to share?"

"Skyd—" He coughed loudly into his fist.

Elle's heart dropped. "Excuse me? What did you just say?"

With a long, drawn-out sigh, Ted looked toward her. Although his eyes settled on something over her left shoulder. "Skydiving. We decided to go skydiving."

Rapidly blinking as her brain tried to process this latest information, Elle opened her mouth, only no words came out.

"It was amazing," he continued. "Nothing like it. What a rush. Of course, once I landed, I got a little winded. No big deal."

"No big deal?" Her voice came out loud and harsh.

At that moment, the door opened behind her and she heard Cam's voice before she saw him. "Everything okay in here?"

"No, no, everything is not okay. In fact, it's pretty far from okay. Do you know what he did today?" She pointed at her father as her voice continued to rise. "Do you know how he ended up in the hospital? He jumped out of a plane with his friends."

Cam's eyebrows shot up and he let out an amused sound. "No kidding? That's awesome."

"Right!" Ted agreed. "I don't know why she's so worked up."

"Worked up?" Elle paced to the window and back. She stabbed a finger in her dad's direction before swinging it at Cam. "Don't encourage him. He is in the hospital."

"And he's fine."

"He shouldn't be doing anything to put him in the position of not being fine," she said.

"The man just dealt with cancer," Cam said.

"Exactly my point." She threw her hands in the air.

"In my opinion, he should get to live a little."

"Oh, really? Well, in my opinion, this is none of your business."

Cam rocked back on his heels. "I think you need to calm down. Look at him. He's fine."

Elle gestured with both hands. Wildly. "We're in a hospital. Does that seem fine to you?" She took a step closer to Cam.

Following suit, he closed the distance between them so that they were nose to nose. "I think he had a little incident and will be home tomorrow."

"Wanna know what I think?" her dad piped up from the bed.

"No," they answered in tandem. Finally, an agreement.

"You need to back off," Cam suggested.

"Back off? I only just found out about the cancer. I've been back a matter of weeks and he's throwing himself out of moving planes. Do you know how worried I've been?" Her voice cracked, but she kept her gaze locked on Cam's.

His smug expression softened. "I do." He ran a hand up her arm. "I'm sorry."

Elle peered into Cam's eyes and saw such kindness there. She wanted to fold herself into his arms and stay that way for a long time. She wished they could beam themselves back to his cabin and return to that couch.

The strangest thing was that she'd experienced sensitivity and understanding with a guy before. And she'd definitely felt her share of lust and longing. But she'd never found one guy who made her feel both.

At that moment, it was a good thing they were in a hospital, because her own heart gave a little flutter.

"So that's settled," her dad called from the bed. Elle jumped back a foot. Yikes, her dad was in the room. "Everybody okay now?"

With her eyes still trained on Cam, she considered the question. Given her recent realization, she was anything but okay. Luckily, a nurse entered the room and asked to see her.

After following her outside the room to the nurses' station, Elle was given a series of forms to fill out. When she was done, the nurse offered an understanding smile.

"Visiting hours are just about over. Please say your goodbyes for the night."

Elle walked back toward her father's room. When she looked inside the window in the door, she saw that her dad had fallen asleep. She watched as Cam covered him with a blanket and turned off the television.

"How are you doing?" he asked when he'd exited the room.

She didn't say anything, because the truth was she wasn't doing all that well. What kind of daughter was never around when the important stuff happened?

"Elle?" Cam pressed. "How are you feeling?"

"Embarrassed." What was it about this man that broke down her usual walls and made her reveal each and every thought in her head? "I'm never here when he needs me," she admitted in a quiet voice. "When he was diagnosed I was a million miles away in Italy. I wasn't here for his first round of treatment."

"He didn't tell you about his illness. You can't blame yourself for that."

Standing up straighter, she shook her head. "If I had lived here I would have known. He could hide the diagnosis from me because I didn't have any way of finding out over in Europe. And today..."

"Was a good day," Cam finished. "You weren't in Italy. You were a little more than an hour away."

"But—"

"And now you're here with him." He pushed a stray hair back from her forehead. "You are allowed to leave for a day. You're a good daughter. Stop feeling guilty."

Something about his tone of voice—or maybe the stubborn look in his eyes—had the sides of her mouth twitching. "You're so bossy."

He winked at her. "Only when I need to be. Now, stop feeling sorry for yourself and let me take you home."

She peeked in the window of her dad's room once more. He was out for the night and she could come back first thing tomorrow morning. After all, he'd said he didn't want her to sleep in the hospital. But if something happened...

"The nurses will call you if anything goes down," Cam said, reading her thoughts.

Nodding silently, she gathered her things and walked down the hallway with him. When they got outside, she took a moment to breathe in the clean, non-hospital-smelling air. Looking up, she saw a sky full of stars twinkling down on them.

She used to look at those same stars in Florence and wonder what was happening in Bayside. She'd wonder if anyone from home missed her or if she'd ever return.

"What are you thinking about?" Cam's voice pulled her out of her thoughts.

"How I keep running away," she said truthfully.

"There's a solution to that, you know."

Even though she was still looking up, she knew he'd turned. She could sense those penetrating eyes on her. Goose pimples spread over her skin. "What's that?"

With a gentle hand, he brought her head down so she had to face him. "Stop running."

It sounded so simple and Elle desperately wished it was. But she knew better. She knew the way this town was.

"I know it's been hard for you. And yesterday was a real pisser of a day. But if you stop fleeing, exist here in Bayside without the threat of leaving again, you might give the town a chance to learn who you are now. They only know the Ellie Owens who ended her time in Bayside with a crazy incident."

"I thought you said that 'incident' was passionate," she teased.

"I said *you* were passionate. Besides, I was trying to get into your pants."

She blushed. "Thanks."

"And I'm still trying." He pulled her against him, encompassing her in his strong arms. She loved when he did that.

Still, she shoved back slightly. "Cam, someone will see."

He didn't respond. Only watched her with a smile on his lips. "I'm going to kiss you now. And you're right, someone might see."

Then his lips were on hers and thinking about someone catching them melted away. The only thought was Cam. She gave herself over to the kiss. Over to him. Elle let herself get carried away in that parking lot because the idea of not kissing Cam seemed equivalent to not breathing.

When he lifted his head, she noticed that his eyes were

cloudy. Dark and stormy and full of passion. They had to mirror her own, if her accelerated heartbeat was any indication.

"I should take you home," he said, his voice gruff.

"Yes, you should." She stared at him, searching his face for the sign she needed. When his eyes dipped to take in her lips, she had her answer. "But…"

"But what?" he quickly asked.

"But it might be better if you take me to your home instead."

Cam studied her for a full second. His grin started slow and ended up being fully delicious. "Yes, ma'am."

Hand in hand, they dashed to his truck. She didn't consider the fact that people could probably see them. She didn't contemplate if this was right or wrong. She didn't even care if the Bayside Blogger reported on this.

The only thought in Elle's head was how fast they could get to Cam's house.

Cam didn't particularly remember driving back to his bungalow after the hospital. He wouldn't be able to tell anyone what he and Elle talked about as they drove through town. And he didn't recall taking Elle's hand and heading up the walkway to his front porch.

But he would never forget the way she looked standing in his living room with the full moon beaming through the window, casting a glow on her beautiful face.

Did she have any idea how gorgeous she was? Cam racked his brain, but honestly couldn't recall meeting a more exquisite woman in his life. And the fact that she was fun to talk to, that she listened attentively and that she could go with the flow only added to her appeal.

He dropped his keys on the table by the front door. Or hell, maybe they missed and fell on the floor. He had no idea. All he knew was that Elle Owens was inside his house, watching him with a knowing smile and a twinkle in her eyes.

Cam considered himself to be a confident man. He felt comfortable in his own skin. But ever since she'd told him to take her to his house, it was as if he was a fumbling teenager again.

It wasn't as if he'd never been with a woman before. Still, something held him in place. He dragged a hand through his hair, at a loss for what to do or what to say.

"You gonna stand way over there all night?" she asked with laughter in her voice.

"Can I get you something to drink? Are you hungry? Do you want a tour of the house?"

Her lips curved, spreading slowly into a devastating smile. Then she crooked her finger at him. "Come here, Cam."

As if on autopilot, he glided across the room, closing the distance between them. Elle wound her arms around his neck. Tilting her head back, she pinned him with a perceptive stare.

"Are you nervous, Cameron?" Before he could answer, she continued. "Because if anyone should be nervous, it should be me."

Her statement snapped him out of his stupor. Wrapping his arms around her tiny waist, he drew her closer to him. "And why would you be nervous?"

She bit her bottom lip briefly before saying, "Because you're Cameron Dumont, old and mysterious loner."

He felt his eyebrow quirk at the description. "Old?"

She grinned. "Yep. That's what I said."

He leaned down and nipped her earlobe. "Nothing wrong with being old." He pressed his lips to the column of her neck. Her throat was sensitive, he'd found. But he kissed it again. She smelled so good there. "Old goes hand in hand with experience."

Her head fell back as he moved his lips up to her jaw-line and around to the other ear. He sucked her earlobe into his mouth. "Experience is good," she said with a ragged breath.

"Then get ready. Because you're about to get a taste of it."

With that, he reached down and scooped her up in his arms. He liked her quick inhalation. Even in the dark, he could see that her face was flushed and he liked the way that looked on her.

Cam quickly made his way down the hallway to his bedroom. But once there, he didn't release her. Instead, he took a moment to relish the feel of Elle in his arms. As he placed a kiss on her forehead, he indulged himself in feeling her silky hair against his skin. Despite driving to and from the cabin, spending a couple hours in an antiseptic-filled hospital and fishing in the lake, she still managed to smell amazing—as if she bathed in flowers.

Bathed in flowers? Oh, man. He was falling hard for Elle Owens. If that thought didn't scare the crap out of him, he would actually laugh at himself. In fact, he couldn't stop a chuckle from escaping now.

"What is it?" she asked, squirming in his arms.

He took one long look into those dreamy green eyes and any anxiety simply melted away. So did his laughter.

"Nothing," he told her.

"Seems like something," she countered.

He answered her with a kiss. A long, intoxicating kiss as he gently set her on the floor. Running his hands through her hair, he pulled her to him so he could deepen the kiss. When she opened her mouth and he slipped his tongue inside, he was surprised to hear a moan. Was even more shocked that it came from him.

When Elle moved her lips to the side of his neck, he let out another groan, but stayed busy by reaching for her shirt. He made quick work of the buttons and pushed the plaid material off her shoulders. Even as she continued her clever work on his neck and jaw, he reached for the bottom of her T-shirt. He pulled it up and over her head.

She stood before him in her lacy pink bra and snug-fitting jeans. It might possibly be the hottest sight he'd ever seen.

She nodded down at her half-clothed body. "You gonna stop there?" Her voice was husky and full of need. He knew the feeling.

Suddenly overtaken by his own want, he felt as if something snapped inside him, and he crushed his mouth to hers. The next few minutes were a blur of undressing each other, with clothes flying around the room as they attempted to continue kissing and touching.

Her bra was nice, but removing it was even better. Ample breasts filled his hands while she yanked at his jeans, finally dropping them to pool around his ankles.

With a laugh, Elle fell backward onto his bed, her hair splaying across his dark blue bedspread. Cam took that as an invitation and covered her with his body. He was down to his boxer briefs.

She pointed a slender finger toward his underwear and the erection that was pulsing to be let free. "Cam?" she asked.

Her eyes had turned a dark forest green. He could see it by the light of the moon shining in through the bedroom window. Her chest was rising and falling. "Yeah?" he groaned out.

She pushed up on her elbows, showcasing her luscious breasts, and gestured to his boxer briefs. "Lose the pants."

Elle couldn't believe this was happening. She was about to see Cam. All of Cam.

Who would have thought?

She shook her head. If she was honest—utterly and brutally honest—this night wasn't a surprise. Her feelings for him had been growing rapidly every day since she'd returned. Even in that first moment when he'd met her in the town square, she'd known. There had been...something. Something that shifted inside her.

She wanted him naked, but decided to help out by going first. Trying to be as seductive as possible, she removed her panties.

His eyes darkened as they swept over her entire body. Slowly, greedily. His breathing picked up, too.

As if in slow motion, she watched as he hooked his thumbs in the waistband of his sexy-as-hell black boxer briefs. Why all guys didn't wear boxer briefs was beyond her.

Her mouth went dry. She wanted to make some kind of nonchalant comment, but there was no way her brain could form words at the moment. Not at the sight of Cam's incredibly impressive erection.

Looking up, she saw that he was watching her—taking in her every movement in that quiet, steady way he had.

"Elle, are you sure?"

It melted her heart that he asked. A safe bet would be that she'd never been surer of anything in her life.

"Cam..." she began. There were so many things she wanted to say, yet at the same time, all she truly wanted was to feel his body on top of hers. She wanted to revel in the sensation of skin on skin and bodies fused together. "Kiss me," she whispered.

Not wasting any time, Cam placed one hand behind her head as he lowered both of them onto the soft mattress. He covered her lips with his as his hands ran over her body. Hands that were rough and callused from work. And that hardness felt amazing. Everywhere they touched tingled.

He had a long day's growth of stubble on his face and

she could feel it rubbing against her skin as he moved his head down her throat and over her collarbone to the swell of her breast. She sucked in an uneven breath as his skillful tongue found her nipple. Arching her back, she pushed herself up to give him better access. After he finished with one breast he moved to the next, and Elle was helpless to do anything but enjoy the sensations as she dug her nails into his back and hung on for dear life.

When he was done with his exploration, he lifted his head and met her eyes. She saw something there. Something she hadn't expected. Something much stronger than simple lust. And whatever that something was, it both exhilarated and scared her.

"Cam, let me—"

He touched a finger to her lips. "No, tonight is for you."

"Oh, well—" Her words cut off when he pressed his lips to her stomach and began a slow descent even lower.

Cam used his lips, his tongue to pleasure her, with each movement he made increasing the need building inside her. When he slipped one finger inside her, she called out his name. But he was relentless, urging her to go higher and higher as he found a sweet rhythm with his mouth.

Just as he touched his thumb to her most sensitive nub, she tensed before crying out again. Then she was falling, and he moved back to nuzzle her neck. The moon seemed to be right outside his bedroom window and was like a spotlight illuminating them as if they were the stars of the entire night.

She reached for his head and brought his lips to hers. The kiss was deep and had her revving up all over again. Cam began to move his erection against her and Elle opened her legs to accommodate him.

"Wait," he said.

Her head flew up. "What?"

With a wry grin, he tapped her nose and sprung off the

bed. He hunched over as he fumbled through the bedside table. Elle quickly realized he was getting a condom. She had been so involved with him that she hadn't thought of it herself.

Protected, Cam positioned himself at the end of the bed. He wrapped his arms around her legs and pulled her to him. He pressed against her opening and slowly, so incredibly slowly, entered her.

She moaned, long and low, at the feel of him inside her, even as her body shifted to accommodate his size. Cam brushed a strand of hair off her face and locked eyes with her.

"Are you okay?"

Biting her lip, she nodded. "Are you?" she asked.

"Yes." His voice was gruff and insanely sexy. "Oh, yes."

And then he began to move. Slowly at first, like silk gliding on top of satin. As they continued to move together, finding a rhythm that worked for both of them, he released her legs and brought his body over hers fully. With hands braced on either side of her head, he increased the tempo.

"Yes, Cam," she called, along with a thousand other incomprehensible words. He answered with moans and grunts as she tightened her grip around his shoulders.

She didn't know how long they moved together as one, but only wished this exquisite feeling could continue forever. She urged him forward by wrapping her legs around his waist, and Cam took advantage of the position by driving into her harder and faster.

Elle could feel the climax building. Just as she was on the ultimate verge, Cam covered her lips with his and pumped into her once, twice, before finally letting go. He was perfectly in tune with her.

And then together they fell from the high, wrapped in each other's arms as the moon shone down on them.

* * *

Well, that had been…really freaking amazing, Cam thought as he snuggled into Elle's warm, soft body.

They'd just finished round two of their night together, and Elle had fallen fast asleep in his arms. He was spooning her now even as her chest rose and fell in a slow rhythm.

He ran a hand over her arm. Her skin was so silky and fresh. Frowning, he noticed the red marks along her face, chin, chest. Probably in other places, as well. More intimate places. It was from his stubble. *Should have shaved*, he thought. Although there was something damn appealing about seeing her body marked by his.

His woman.

Whoa. Cam almost shot up in bed at the notion. But he didn't want to disturb Elle.

What would she do if she heard him call her his woman? Cam didn't need to think hard, because he knew exactly how she'd react. She'd fly out of his life faster than his new chain saw could cut through a tree.

Since she was asleep at the moment, though, he indulged himself by pulling her even closer. He draped an arm over her waist and splayed his fingers over her stomach.

Elle had been back in Bayside a short time, yet she'd been through so much. Not to mention what she'd gone through back in high school.

Cam's temper flared when he thought about those idiotic, mean girls and how they'd gotten her drunk. And yet Elle had never told on them. She'd kept that secret and let herself be ridiculed. That entire night could have ended a lot worse.

Cam wanted her to speak up for herself. He wanted her to give a big middle finger to the entire town. He wanted her to write an op-ed for that stupid blogger she was always worried about.

She murmured in her sleep, a cute sound that had his heart clutching.

He liked being with her. Not just the sex although that had obviously been phenomenal. Just being around her. And he wanted to do it more. Usually, Cam was pretty secretive in relationships. Not because he had anything to hide, but more because he didn't feel the need to put himself out there. What he did behind closed doors was his business only.

For the first time in his life, he actually wanted to stroll down Main Street, hand in hand with his woman. It wouldn't be so bad to go out to eat and attend the different festivals Bayside held throughout the year.

Cam knew Elle wouldn't stick up for herself. At least, not yet. Until she did, any hope of "going public" as a couple was out of the question.

He groaned and Elle stirred. He tightened his hold on her.

Cam would just have to take matters into his own hands. If she wasn't ready to accept him as her boyfriend in public, then he would show her in private what she was missing.

He would make her realize how great it could be between them. And surely she would come around.

Elle woke up to the sound of birds chirping. The window was open and she could feel the morning breeze dancing along her arm. A slice of sunlight entered through that same window, warming her face even as she squinted her eyes at the intrusion of light.

She'd been dreaming. A wonderful, comforting dream that had filled her with happiness and contentment. A dream that had featured Cameron Dumont in a repeat performance of last night.

She couldn't stop the smile from spreading.

Cam.

She quickly cataloged the previous evening. Every touch, every kiss, every moan flashed through her thoughts the way sports shows did those postgame montages.

She bit her lip and timidly rolled over to face him. But to her dismay—and disappointment—the other side of the bed was empty. Strange, she remembered falling asleep in his arms, as his fingers brushed up and down her arm and his warm breath tickled her neck. Normally, Elle was a light sleeper, but she must have really been tired to sleep through him rising.

Of course, she had a pretty good reason for being tired. Her smile grew and she had to hold a laugh back from bubbling up in her throat. Instead, she stretched, her arms going overhead and her legs stiffening as she pointed and flexed her toes.

But where was the source of her morning-after happiness? She glanced at the clock on the end table. She knew that he had multiple jobs going at the same time. She wondered which one he was working on today and how early he had to leave.

Just then, she heard a noise and sat up in bed. Quickly realizing she wasn't wearing any clothes, she pulled the sheet up to cover herself. Before the door opened, she tried to run a hand through her hair, although she knew that was useless. She could feel the knots and tangles.

And then Cam entered the room and she instantly forgot whatever she'd just been obsessing over.

He'd pulled on a pair of sweatpants that hung loosely around his waist. Her mouth watered at the sight of his bare chest and the dark hair that trailed down into the waistband. She'd been running her lips over that trail only hours earlier.

Cam paused in the doorway and even from across the room she could see his eyes darken. He ran his gaze over her and she tightened her hold on the sheet, which was barely covering her chest.

"Good morning," she said, surprised to hear her voice sound husky.

"You're a sight," he said.

"So are you," she countered, and offered a smile. It was only then that she noticed he wasn't empty-handed. He was holding a tray piled with food. Elle couldn't believe she hadn't honed in on the coffee aroma. Normally, caffeine was the first thing on her mind when she woke.

"What's all that?" she asked.

"Breakfast." He walked toward the bed and set the tray down next to her. "I realize it's early, but I get up at this time for work. And I didn't want you to leave hungry."

Touched, Elle took in the spread. Fluffy scrambled eggs, toast, butter, jelly and coffee. Cam had even thought to bring the newspaper inside.

"Cam…wow."

He shrugged as if his effort was nothing.

She reached over and covered his hand with hers. Elle didn't want to make him uncomfortable, but she did want him to realize she appreciated it. "Thank you."

He answered by covering her mouth with his. She wasn't sure if he'd meant for the kiss to be light and airy, but as soon as their lips touched, Elle's entire body woke up and began to tingle with awareness. With need.

She moaned as his lips roamed over hers and his arms encircled her, pulling her in close. He ran light kisses down the column of her neck. The sensation felt amazing. Greedy, Elle tightened her grip on his arms and pulled him down to her.

Buzzzz...

Their heads snapped up at the sound. Cam touched his forehead to hers. "Sorry," he muttered against her mouth. He reached behind her and the buzzing sound stopped. "My alarm."

Elle stole another glance at the clock on the table. It was at that moment that she realized Cam had woken up earlier than he usually did just to make breakfast for her.

"I can't believe you did all this. God, you must have only slept a couple hours."

Again he shrugged. Then he planted a chaste kiss on her lips. "It was worth it to see the smile on your face."

Damn. It was a good thing she was already sitting down because there was no way she would have been able to stand after that comment.

"Listen, I've gotta get to the site. But stay as long as you want. Enjoy breakfast, go back to sleep, whatever you need."

"A girl could get used to this kind of treatment."

He didn't answer her, but Elle thought she saw something in his eyes. A glint of amusement? Awareness? Cockiness? She wasn't sure.

But as Cam gave her one last smoldering glance over his shoulder and exited the room, Elle had the distinct impression that he had somehow gained the upper hand.

Chapter Thirteen

Happy Monday, Bayside! Rumor has it that former Chief of Police Ted Owens was admitted to Bayside Memorial last night. My sources tell me he is going to be just fine. How is his prodigal daughter handling this latest setback? Maybe someone wants to offer her a shoulder to cry on? Oh, wait, seems as if someone already has...

The next night, Elle strolled into Max's Bar and Grill, which sat right off the town square. The decor was rustic, with dark wood, open rafters and a long bar in the middle of the room. There were high tables in the bar area and dozens of tables in the dining area. There were also dartboards on one wall and an old pool table on the other side of the bar.

She'd brought her father home from the hospital that morning and quickly learned that dads made the worst patients. He wanted a vanilla milkshake. She forced him to drink herbal tea. He wanted to watch ESPN. Elle convinced him to take a nap instead. Needless to say, she was thrilled when Riley texted her, asking after her dad and suggesting they grab drinks at Max's.

Elle bit her lip. Maybe she was even more glad, because Riley's invitation came right on the heels of one from Cam. After reading the Bayside Blogger's column earlier in the day, Elle wasn't quite ready to go public with him. Riley gave her the out she needed. Now she was feeling massively guilty.

Needing to do something while she waited for her friend, she pulled up her email on her phone. To her surprise, she saw a message from someone with a Smithsonian handle. Her heart rate picked up as she clicked on the message.

After reviewing your résumé and qualifications, we would love to have you come in for an interview for the position of assistant curator of our European collection.

Elle froze. This position had been at the very top of her wish list. But anything at the Smithsonian was ultra-competitive, so she'd assumed she didn't stand a chance.

Grinning, she reread the email and quickly shot back a note acknowledging that she'd received it and was more than happy to come in for an interview. She even did a little happy dance in her seat after she hit Send. Then her smile suddenly faded.

The job was in Washington, DC, a couple hours from Bayside. A couple hours from the father she'd just reunited with. From Riley and all the new business Elle had drummed up, thanks to her work at Carson's house.

But most important, it was a couple hours from Cam.

Tapping her fingers on the table, she stared at the front door intently. She was ready to burst and desperately needed someone to talk to.

Twenty minutes later, Riley flew inside, spotted Elle and rushed in her direction, even while waving to someone at the bar. Today she wore an adorable turquoise wrap dress and nude heels. Her hair was pulled back in a low ponytail, which accentuated her long neck and a killer statement necklace made up of an array of multicolored stones.

"Sorry, sorry, I know I'm late. But I have a really good excuse." Riley hung her purse on the back of the tall bar stool and hopped up on the seat. "Crazy day. Stupid Mondays. It should have been quiet in the office, but then there was this whole thing that happened in Marketing and Sasha called out sick, and of course Sawyer was all over me to pick up the slack. I mean, it's not like I don't do enough. Trust me, I do plenty. And besides, just because Sawyer is technically my boss doesn't mean that he has to be all uppity with me all the time."

"I had sex with Cam!" Elle blurted out, and then quickly covered her face with her hands. After a moment of complete silence, she peeked through her fingers and saw that Riley's mouth was hanging open.

"Do we need some drinks here?" a chipper waitress asked.

"Hell, yeah," Riley said, waking up from her shock. "Two glasses of pinot and keep 'em coming."

Once the waitress was out of earshot, Riley leaned toward Elle. "I like surprises as much as the next girl, but you gotta give me a little heads-up. I think I just had a heart attack."

"You? How about me? I'm the one who had sex."

"Yes, and I would have thought that act would have mellowed you considerably."

"Sorry," Elle sighed. "I just had to get that out."

Both of them remained quiet as the waitress delivered their wine and offered menus. She said something about a Monday night burger special, but Elle couldn't concentrate on food. In fact, she couldn't even remember if she'd eaten anything since her breakfast in bed, courtesy of Cam.

Cam…

She wondered what he was doing right now. It had been wrong—so freaking wrong—to blow him off tonight. But she'd just…what?

Riley was watching her closely, her emerald-green

eyes offering a knowing sparkle as she tilted her head and pointed a finger at Elle. "You're freaking out, aren't you?"

"Oh, my God." Elle dropped her head onto the table, but could hear Riley chuckle.

"I have a couple questions for you. Please answer all of them, but in no particular order."

Elle straightened and took in her friend as Riley began to tick them off on her fingers.

"How did this happen? Where did it happen? Why aren't you with him right now? And the most important question…" she paused for dramatic effect "…was it good?" She wiggled her eyebrows.

Elle exhaled a long breath that did nothing to relax her. Then she tackled each question in rapid succession. "I have no idea. His place. I'm a chicken. And OMG, stars exploded throughout the universe."

The waitress chose that moment to show up again. "Is there anything else I can get you ladies right now?"

"A cold shower," Riley muttered under her breath.

Elle stifled a laugh. "We're fine. Thanks."

"Okay, let's divide and conquer. I thought your dad went to the hospital last night."

Elle took a long swig of her wine. Then she told Riley everything that had happened the day before.

"Wow, just wow. Okay, first of all, how sweet is Cam for taking you to that cabin? You know, he's never taken a woman there before."

Elle sat up. "How do you know that?"

"How else? The Bayside Blogger reported it once." Riley sat back in her chair and fiddled with her necklace. "He must really like you."

She could feel her cheeks heating up. "Well, I…"

"It was also adorable that he waited at the hospital for you. And then breakfast in bed, when he already has to get up so early for work. Jeez, Elle, you should be on cloud nine today."

"I know, but—"

"And that brings me to the chicken answer. Don't get me wrong, I can always go for some good old-fashioned girl talk."

"But?" Elle arched a brow.

"Seriously, girl. Men like Cam Dumont don't just fall from trees. Trust me, I've been back in Bayside for a couple years and have stood under my fair share of branches." Riley held up her ring finger. "I have nothing to show for it."

Elle giggled. But she quickly grew serious. "It's complicated, Riley."

"So let's talk about it."

"I'm not ashamed of what Cam and I did. Not by a long shot. I just don't want this information to get out there."

Riley frowned. "You mean, out there on a certain blog?"

Elle nodded. "I feel like I have so many eyes on me as it is. I don't want any more attention. Especially when I don't know where this thing with Cam will go. Or if it will go anywhere."

"Why wouldn't it go somewhere?" Riley asked, and gestured to the waitress for two more glasses of wine. "Cam isn't exactly the love-'em-and-leave-'em type."

"But I might be," Elle admitted.

Riley's eyebrows shot so far up her forehead that they were practically on top of her adorable sparkly headband. "What are you talking about? I don't want to slut shame you or anything, but you can't just sleep with Cam and disappear."

"I don't plan on doing that." Elle paused. "Slut shaming?"

"It means…never mind, doesn't matter. The point is, you can't abandon Cam."

"I received an email today. I got a job interview. A really great job."

"Hi, conversation change." Riley laughed.

"Now you know how I feel when I'm with you," Elle teased. "The job is at one of the Smithsonian museums in DC."

"But what about your dad? Isn't he the reason you came back to Bayside?"

"Yeah, he is. But being only a couple hours away is a lot better than living an entire ocean away. Besides, the person in the position now is retiring and that won't happen for a couple months. So I'd still have some time here before I had to move up there."

Riley's face filled with understanding. And if Elle wasn't mistaken, disappointment. "So you slept with Cam last night and now you have an interview for a really great job that just happens to be a couple hours away?"

"That sums it up."

"It's a pickle." Riley accepted her second glass of wine from the waitress and took a long sip as Elle filled her in on the specifics of the position. "The job sounds perfect for you," she offered supportively.

Elle couldn't miss the wistfulness in Riley's voice. She was pretty sure people outside on the street couldn't miss it. "Riley, what gives?"

"I like having you around. It's nice having a friend."

Elle's eyes widened at the statement. "What are you talking about? You have tons of friends." Didn't she? "You know everyone in town."

"True. I am the social butterfly of Bayside." She did a little diva pose with one hand behind her head and her lips puckered into a cute pout. It made Elle laugh. Then her face fell. "I know a lot of people. I have a ton of acquaintances. But you're the only person who really listens to me. And I love hearing about you, too. I'm so glad you came back to town."

Tears prickled behind Elle's eyes. The truth was that Elle loved having a friend, too. She supposed they could still keep in touch if she left, but it wouldn't be the same.

An idea came to her suddenly. It wouldn't solve any problems, but it would make for a fun distraction. A diversion from the possibility of leaving her new friend, from being the main gossip item and, most important, from having to deal with Cam.

"Can you get a day or two off work this week?"

"I don't know. Maybe. Why, what's up?"

"Well, my interview is on Wednesday. Why don't we road trip up to DC, be tourists on Wednesday and stay overnight? An impromptu girls trip. What do you think?"

Riley smiled. "I think I love everything about this idea."

"Great. I'll make all the arrangements." She reached for her cell phone to make some notes. Riley put her hand over Elle's, getting her attention.

"Just do me a favor," her friend began. "Talk to Cam before we leave. Let him know how you're feeling."

"I…" She trailed off because she didn't know what to say.

"He deserves that much, at least," Riley said quietly.

No, he deserved a hell of a lot more than that, which was exactly what Elle was afraid of. Because she wasn't sure she was ready to give.

Elle returned home to find her father asleep and the rest of the house quiet. Yet she couldn't seem to settle. She stretched out on her old childhood bed and thought about what Riley had said earlier.

Cam deserved to know how she was feeling.

But what if he didn't understand? What if he didn't

agree? What if…he was standing at her bedroom window his hand poised to knock?

Elle let out a little yelp at seeing Cam's grinning face reflected through her half-open window. "Cam!" She quickly glanced back at the door, hoping her dad hadn't woken up.

Cam chuckled as she walked toward the window and opened it all the way. "What are you doing here?"

Her stomach instantly became a mass of nerves at the rugged stubble on his face. At the casual jeans and T-shirt he wore. At the sight of his handsome eyes sweeping over her body.

Her body was currently covered in an old Bayside High T-shirt and decade-old boxer shorts. Not to mention her hair was piled haphazardly on top of her head and she'd scrubbed all the makeup from her face.

In defense mode, she grabbed her light blue curtain and twisted it around her, hiding in the cocoon.

He chuckled. "What are you doing?"

"You can't see me like this," she uttered from behind her thin layer of protection.

Before she could react, his arm snapped out and grabbed her waist. He used that big palm to push her body until she spun in a circle and unwound herself from the curtain.

Elle bowed her head, but Cam's finger went under her chin, forcing her to meet his gaze.

"You look beautiful."

Funny how three little words could have the butterflies start up in her belly. She felt like a teenager again. "Do you want to come in or do you want to continue to gawk at me through the window?"

"I'm fine here." He pulled her hand to his lips and brushed a kiss over her knuckles. Her toes curled and she sucked in a sharp breath. "I missed you today." With that, he kissed her, and all those nerves simply dissipated as if they'd never been there to begin with.

He smiled. "I liked last night. I liked it a lot. I want to do it again."

It was her turn to smile. "Right here? Right now?"

He sat on the windowsill and gave a little nod toward her bedroom door. "I don't think your dad would appreciate finding me on top of his daughter in her childhood bedroom. Do you?"

"Who said you'd get to be on top?"

Cam's eyes darkened and he let out a very masculine growl.

"Cam," she began.

After giving her a quick once-over, he asked, "Are you having second thoughts about last night?"

His expression was serious and his dark eyes hesitant. But he continued to hold her hand, his fingers steady and sure as they wrapped around hers. His skin was rough and callused and she instantly remembered what it had felt like when it ran over her body last night. With her palm engulfed in his grip, she felt safe and protected.

Leaning forward, she pressed her lips to his. "No, I'm not having second thoughts," she told him. "Last night was amazing and I'm glad it happened, too."

His shoulders relaxed, as did his face. "Good." He leaned back against the frame of the window. "So what's this I hear about you and Riley leaving town?" He raised an eyebrow.

"Riley and... But how did you..."

He nodded, an amused expression on his face.

"The Bayside Blogger knows that Riley and I are going to DC this week?"

Cam frowned. "This week?"

"Oh. Well, it's just..." Cam straightened and a lump

formed in Elle's throat. She'd upset him. "We're only going for a day and a half."

He studied her. "You didn't mention it."

"We only just decided tonight at dinner."

She could smell him. Even with the distance he'd just put between them, his earthy, woodsy aroma wafted over to her, like clean, fresh laundry on top of recently chopped pine.

This would be the time to tell him the real reason she and Riley were heading up to DC. She needed to come clean about the job interview. She opened her mouth, but no words came out.

"There's something else, isn't there?" Cam asked.

It felt like he was reading her every thought. She didn't quite understand it, but Elle didn't want to tell him about the interview yet. Her earlier conversation with Riley played through her mind and she knew her friend was right. Cam deserved to know everything. Especially after last night.

Of course, she might not get the job. In that case, she would have possibly upset him for nothing. And yet she knew that was a cop-out, as well.

So she told him something else that was true instead. "I'm worried about the Bayside Blogger," she blurted.

"Elle," Cam said, sounding exasperated. "No one cares about that loony tune."

"Plenty of people care. You care." She pointed at him. "You knew that Riley and I are going to DC."

"First of all, I do not read her column or her tweets or twits or whatever. My mom, on the other hand, does follow her, and she told me about the trip to DC. And second, so what? You don't want people to know that the two of us are together? You're embarrassed to be associated with the likes of a mere contractor?"

What? No, of course she didn't feel that way. She felt

awful that he even had to say that. But then she saw the twinkle in his eyes. "Cameron Dumont," she said.

"Elle Owens," he replied.

"Of course I'm not embarrassed to be around you. It's just that I don't want any undue gossip filtering around town about me."

He held up his hand. "I understand, Elle."

She tilted her head. "You do?"

"I get that it's been rough for you since you got back. And hell, we don't know where this thing between us is going to go. So if it will make you more comfortable, let's keep it quiet for a while."

It seemed too good to be true. "Seriously?"

"Yeah. But only for a short time. I won't be your dirty little secret forever."

She laughed right before she nipped his bottom lip. "Ohh…" she purred into his ear, before biting there, as well. "Dirty little secrets are the best kind."

His arms wrapped around her and his lips were fused to hers instantly. The kiss took her breath away.

"I should probably be going," he said, when they broke apart.

"Mmm, probably." She licked her lips, reveling in the taste that was purely Cam. When she met his gaze, his eyes had clouded over.

"Keep doing that and I'm definitely staying. Definitely getting you in trouble with your dad."

She laughed, and he reached out and tucked a lock of hair behind her ear. Then he said, "Now that our dirty little secret has been taken care of, why don't we try dinner tomorrow? I know a place about twenty miles from here that you'll love."

"Sounds great," she said, and meant it.

Only the look on Cam's face said otherwise. Apparently, it didn't sound great to him. Peering closer, she saw a dark shadow there. She cast her eyes downward, but when she looked up again, Cam's normal stoic expression was firmly back in place.

He kissed her soundly on the lips and whispered, "See you tomorrow," before retreating into the night, leaving Elle feeling the same way she had at the beginning of the evening.

Very, very guilty.

Chapter Fourteen

Guess what, Bayside! We just got our favorite little gossip item back and it seems Ellie Owens might be leaving us for greener pastures in the nation's capital. *Gasp* Say it ain't so, Ellie! Even more interesting is the person who will be really upset by the departure of little Ellie. And it ain't her father...

Cam was having a real pisser of a day. One of those mornings where every little thing seemed to go wrong, from waking up late to bringing the wrong blueprints to forgetting his lunch.

That said nothing of his bad attitude and foul mood. His crew had been either tiptoeing around him or avoiding him completely.

Fine by Cam. He didn't feel like chatting.

Stepping back to study a particularly pesky piece of wood that needed a very specific measurement, he sighed. The truth was there actually was someone he'd like to chat with.

He'd like to do a hell of a lot more with her, too.

Damn, it had been only two days and he missed her. No, he thought, shaking his head. He craved her.

There was no doubt he'd been attracted to Elle since the day she stepped off that airport shuttle. But each day, everything about her, from her gorgeous looks to her amazing personality, infiltrated his usually well-guarded control more and more. Now all he could do was wait around for her to return from DC.

Since this was the first time Cam Dumont had ever waited for any female to do anything, he didn't know how to handle the feeling. So he indulged his sour mood and whacked a piece of scrap wood with his hammer.

"What did that wood ever do to you?"

"Shut up," he answered his little brother.

Unlike his crew, Jasper was undeterred at Cam's biting words. He hopped down into the pit where Cam was working.

"Rough morning, cupcake?"

Cam glared at him. "What are you even doing here?"

"Come on," Jasper cooed, as if Cam were some cranky toddler. "What's wrong? You can tell me."

With a quick once-over, Cam took in Jasper's gray suit, purple shirt and complementing purple tie, black Ray-Ban sunglasses and shoes that probably cost more than Cam was making on this job. His brother should, by all accounts, seem completely out of place among the tools and equipment, the mounds of dirt and scrap material. Yet Jasper had that way of fitting in everywhere.

"I've heard you've been a real peach this morning," he said conversationally.

"Who the hell said that?" Cam asked.

Jasper sauntered over to Cam's workspace and glanced at it, as if he knew what he was looking at. "You've managed to piss off the majority of your crew. What gives?"

Cam answered by shrugging.

Jasper sighed. "This delightful mood wouldn't have anything to do with Ellie Owens, would it?"

Cam made a rude gesture at his brother, then pushed his safety goggles on top of his head.

Laughing, Jasper held his hands up in a show of surrender. "Okay, okay. I'll stop messing around. Besides, I did stop by to see if you wanted to grab lunch. I have something to discuss about our project and you're not going to be happy."

"Super."

Cam and Jasper were renovating some storefront commercial properties in the center of town near the water. It was a bit of a passion project for both of them, but had come with many hiccups.

After Cam cleaned up his space—and himself—Jasper led him toward his car and they both hopped in. After a short ride, they pulled up in front of Max's Bar and Grill.

Once they were seated, burgers ordered and Cam had taken his first long gulp of cold, refreshing water, he noticed his brother lean back and assess him. "What?" Cam asked.

"Nothing. Just making sure you're really okay."

"Why wouldn't I be? Just in a bad mood today. Nothing to write home about."

"So Elle…" Jasper trailed off, fiddling with his paper napkin.

"Was only gone for two days. In fact, she should be back already."

Jasper gave him a quizzical look. "You haven't heard?"

"About?" Cam asked, as the waitress refilled his water glass.

He noticed that Jasper waited until she was out of earshot, then leaned forward. "Her job interview."

Cam grinned. "Elle got an interview? That's great." He couldn't wait to see her and congratulate her in person. But Jasper's face remained serious.

"Cam, the job is in DC."

The waitress showed up again and placed plates with large loaded burgers and a mountain of fries in front of them. "Hope you guys are hungry."

With the sudden twisting going on in his stomach, Cam could safely say he was categorically not hungry.

"You didn't know," Jasper observed.

He shook his head. "How did you find out?"

His brother reached over to the table next to them and grabbed a copy of the *Bayside Bugle* someone had left. He rifled through the pages and finally folded one back and slapped it in front of Cam.

Cam gritted his teeth. "That freaking Blogger."

"Yep," Jasper agreed. "That freaking Blogger says Elle is up for some position at the Smithsonian in DC."

Scanning the article, Cam shoved a fry in his mouth, but it tasted like sawdust. He didn't even flinch at the fact that it was way too hot.

"Well, good for her. That job sounds like it's right up her alley."

"Cam," Jasper began.

"What the hell is there to say? Elle and I aren't anything to each other. Just because we've slept together..."

"Excuse me, what?"

But he ignored his brother. "I thought I was doing the right thing."

"By sleeping with her?" Jasper asked, blowing on one his fries before popping it into his mouth. "Nothing wrong with that as long as she was willing."

Cam pegged him with a seriously-stop-messing-with-me look. "Of course she was willing." The mere thought of how willing Elle had been as he'd moved over her, under her, inside her, had Cam readjusting the way he was sitting. "That's not what I'm talking about."

Jasper lifted a brow and waited.

"She doesn't want our relationship getting out there because of this damn Blogger person." He flicked the newspaper.

Jasper chortled. "Sounds perfect for you. I don't remember the last time you openly dated someone."

Cam jutted a finger toward his brother. "Exactly. I usually like flying under the radar. But with Elle..."

Jasper nodded, understanding flooding his face. "You like her, Cam. Really like her. It's refreshing to see."

"Yeah, well, hell of a lot of good that does me if she's interviewing for a job hours away."

Jasper added ketchup to his fries. "It was only an interview. She might not get the job."

"Of course she'll get it. You should see this mural she did for one of my clients. Un-freaking-believable."

After taking a large bite of his burger and washing it down with a swig of Coke, Jasper sat back and seemed to consider something. "You don't want Elle to leave Bayside, right?"

His first instinct was to brush off the question. But the truth was Cam desperately wanted Elle to stick around. He wanted to spend more time with her—in and out of bed.

"Yeah," he answered.

"Then you need to give her a reason to stay."

Cam dropped the burger he'd finally picked up. "What are you saying?"

Jasper took another bite and then wiped his mouth before continuing. "Elle needs a job. But she had to go all the way to DC to find one. Make that easier on her." To emphasize his point, he tapped the briefcase he'd carted into the bar.

It was as if a lightbulb went on. Cam knew exactly what his brother had in mind and he felt like an idiot for not thinking of it himself.

"You follow?" Jasper asked.

He nodded emphatically and finally took a hearty bite of his burger, savoring the taste. "I do. Not a bad idea. You know, sometimes you're kinda smart."

"I thought I was annoying?" Jasper said with a grin.

"That, too. Although the level of annoyance will depend on what you have to tell me about our project. How bad is it?"

Jasper grimaced.

"Am I gonna need a beer to hear this?"

"You're gonna need a beer and a shot."

Cam sat back and steeled himself, ready to talk shop. But in the back of his mind, he couldn't help but relax. Jasper had come up with a great idea. It would entice Elle to stick around and had the added bonus of clearing up Cam's bad mood.

It should have been an amazing time.

Elle grabbed her cappuccino from The Brewside and went to one of the tables that had recently been placed outside. The weather had gotten warmer and the sun was reflecting off the bay.

She looked that way now. It had rained last night and the water was still a bit choppy. Birds were diving into the waves in search of food. A boat was in the process of docking.

She'd liked visiting the nation's capital. But the crazy traffic, the inherent commotion of urban living and the crowds of people were so different than Bayside.

She and Riley had gone to the National Gallery, walked along the Mall and watched the sun set over the monuments. They'd visited Georgetown and ate an amazing dinner on M Street. Not to mention the shopping.

At night they'd found a fun piano bar and sung loudly as they drank gin and tonics. Riley seemed in her element amid the hustle and bustle of city life. She'd kept pointing out different aspects of DC that Elle would get to enjoy if she landed the job and moved there.

The interview had gone incredibly well. She met with Will Mitchum, the curator of the Hirshhorn Museum and

Sculpture Garden, one of the seventeen Smithsonian Museums. They wanted to expand their European collection and Mr. Mitchum told her that the Smithsonian would be lucky to hire someone with her experience in the art world.

And yet Elle sat outside The Brewside now, with her drink untouched and her stomach in knots.

Riley had noticed her unease on the drive back home. But she'd said only one quick comment.

"You don't have to take the job if they offer it."

But Elle knew she would be an idiot not to accept such a perfect position. The job combined everything she loved about the art world.

Elle thought about her dad, who looked much better after his brief stint in the hospital. He was excited for her. And she'd be able to get back to Bayside on the weekends. If something really bad happened she could drive home in a matter of hours.

But I won't be here every day.

That was the real concern. Elle couldn't help but feel selfish. She should be thinking predominantly about her dad—and she was—but there was someone else who had managed to worm his way into her thoughts.

Cam.

Right on cue, she saw him entering the square and walking in the opposite direction of The Brewside. His long legs ate up the distance in quick strides. He was on a mission.

Coffee completely forgotten now, Elle stood up so fast that the table wobbled as she headed off to catch up with him. There were a few storefronts on this end of the square that weren't currently occupied. It looked like they'd been newly renovated, Elle thought. She could smell the distinctive aromas of fresh paint and recently cut wood.

Cam stopped in front of one of the stores and let out an oath.

"Hey," Elle called.

He spun around, a sour look on his face, and his fingers clenched into tight fists. She put her hands up in front of her in a show of surrender.

"Sorry." He shook his head.

"Rough day?" she asked.

"Annoying day." But his face softened as he took her in. He reached out, then let his hand fall. "Sorry, wanted to…"

He wanted to what? She glanced around the square, but no one was paying attention to them. Elle took advantage by throwing her arms around him and pressing her face into his neck. He smelled like Cam, and she quickly realized that in only two short days she'd come to miss that smell.

After a swift kiss, she stepped back. He watched her, an incredulous look on his face. "I thought you weren't going to do that in public."

She waved her hand nonchalantly, even though her eyes darted around the square again. "I just wanted to."

"You just wanted to," he repeated. "How was DC? Did you and Riley have a good time?"

Elle smiled. "We did." She twisted her hands together in an effort to keep them from fidgeting. "Actually, I should tell you something."

Cam leaned back against the building. "Oh, yeah? What's that?"

"I went to DC for another reason. I had a job interview at the Smithsonian. I'm sorry. I should have told you about it before I left."

"You're telling me about it now." He reached out and stroked her cheek.

"You're not mad?" Even she could hear the surprise in her voice.

Cam opened his mouth, but quickly closed it. Instead, he studied her from the top of her head down to her casual sneakers. "You look beautiful."

Flustered, she ran a hand over her hair and blushed. She was wearing a pair of tight jeans and a pink flowy blouse. She had on the minimum amount of makeup, although she was happy she'd remembered to apply her favorite shimmering pink lip gloss. In any case, Elle knew she didn't look spectacular in any way.

"You're funny," she said in way of a reply. "What were you swearing about when I came up just now?"

His eyebrows drew together again and he let out a loud groan. "My brother and I have a pet project." He gestured behind him to four of the shops. "This end of the square has sat unoccupied for a couple years now."

Elle glanced around. The stores in question were in a great location, overlooking the bay yet right in the middle of town. "I would have thought people would be lined up to have their businesses here."

"That's what Jasper thought, too. He looked into it. He found two interesting items. First of all, the guy who owned all of these commercial spaces raised the rent every single year. And I'm not talking a small amount. But the other issue was far more worrying. This building in particular hadn't been updated in decades. The place was falling apart."

"Again, I'm shocked that no one in town knew this," Elle offered.

"Turns out the guy had a friend on the town council. That friend is no longer serving good ole Bayside. Jasper bought this area."

Elle's mouth fell open. "Your family owns the town square?"

"Well, my brother and I own these buildings. A major point of contention between Jasper and my parents. But I think it was a great business decision. Besides, his heart was in the right place."

"Where do you fit into all of this?"

"Jasper hired me to bring everything up to code. With these four properties, we had to do some major renovations. Which brings me to my bad mood. The owner for this store—" he pointed at the building directly behind him "—pulled out."

"What do you mean? They're not going to open their business?"

"Apparently not. Paying the penalty and everything. We're going to hold a big grand opening for the new and improved square. I really wanted the whole area to be occupied when we did that, even if the individual stores weren't ready to open. Damn jewelry shop." Cam kicked at a stone on the ground.

They turned toward the building now. Elle could feel the tension coming off him. "I like this space," she said, peering inside. "There's so much natural light."

He nodded and pulled out a key chain with about thirty different keys hanging off it. "Come on, I'll show you around."

They entered the store and Elle took in the dark wooden floors and pristine walls. There were large windows that had clearly been installed recently.

"You mentioned natural light," Cam said. "The whole place is designed for that feature. In the evening, it will overlook the sunset across the bay." He pointed.

She glanced in that direction now. It was close to sunset and the sky had already begun to change colors. Elle's trained artistic eye took in the hues and shading. "Wow, that's going to be spectacular."

"Looks like it's going to be nothing at the moment."

"That's really too bad. I can totally envision it. Displays could hang over there." She pointed toward the right side of the large room.

"Oh, yeah?" Cam sounded amused.

"Well, if I were setting it up, I would use this entire wall for artwork, give the place some color and life."

Elle noticed that Cam was watching her intensely as she walked around the space. "What?" she asked, feeling self-conscious.

"You should set up this space."

Not understanding, she stayed quiet and walked toward the built-in counter, no doubt the cashier station. Running a hand along the sanded wood painted a fresh, crisp shade of white, she couldn't help but admire the workmanship.

"Elle, you should open a gallery here."

She did a double take. "What?"

"Isn't that what you did in Italy? You ran a gallery. Why not do that here? You've been looking for work."

"I can't afford to open my own business."

"That's what business loans are for. I can walk you through the whole process. I've been through it myself," he added eagerly.

It was a ridiculous idea, she thought as she turned away from Cam and walked farther into the space. Although she'd be lying if she claimed it wasn't an interesting idea to entertain.

The front room was perfect for displaying art. She could even dedicate a section to local artists. The back room was huge, but could probably be split into two. One side for packaging and mailing, and the other for a studio. Wouldn't it be interesting to rent it out to artists and have a glass wall so customers could watch them work?

Of course, she would probably have to portion off another section, too. After all, she'd need an office.

She groaned. What was she doing? She couldn't open a gallery here. Or anywhere.

Could she?

"You're intrigued."

She turned at the sound of Cam's voice, surprised that

she was standing in the far corner. How long had she been back here?

"I'm… I don't know what I am."

"You're second-guessing yourself, that's what you're doing." He walked over and took her hand. "Stop thinking of all the reasons you shouldn't or couldn't do this. Start thinking about the possibilities."

She clamped her lips shut, because she wanted to tell him to forget about it. This was a crazy idea. A really stupid, insane, irrational idea. Elle wasn't in the habit of making unreasonable decisions, especially when the rate of failure was so high.

So why did it feel really, really right?

Gnawing on her lower lip, she spun in a circle. Everywhere she looked, she could so clearly imagine a transformed space.

But she'd just had that interview in Washington, DC. For a really amazing job. Her dream job.

A dream job that didn't include her dad, or her hometown…or Cam.

"It feels damn good to run your own business."

She looked up when he spoke again. He'd shoved his hands into the front pockets of his well-worn jeans. For the first time since she'd met him—or returned from Italy and remet him—Cam seemed unsure.

"You put all of yourself into building it, maintaining it, fostering it. Your blood, sweat and tears keep you going through the rough times," he continued. "But no matter what happens, you know that you've built something special."

Something that didn't have anything to do with Jasper or that damn video. Something that would be all hers. And Bayside would finally see that she was a normal human being. Elle would finally be able to shed the image of little Ellie Owens and her crazy behavior.

Cam ran a hand along his jaw. "Look, I know you just had an interview for some great job. DC has a lot to offer. I'm not going to downplay that."

She stepped toward him. "What are you doing, then?"

He closed the distance and framed her face with his big, strong hands. "I'm pleading with you to consider an alternate idea. DC is not the only option." He nipped her lip before brushing his mouth over hers.

A shiver went through her and she wound her arms around his neck. His mouth was on hers again. She parted her lips and let him take what he needed.

Why are you pushing this idea?

She didn't ask it because she thought she already knew the answer. Cam wanted her to stay in Bayside.

Elle didn't know how she felt about that. The only thing she knew right now was that she was wrapped around his hard body and she could feel his erection against her stomach.

She knew that they were making out in a semipublic place.

She knew that she wanted to do more than merely "think" about his idea to open a gallery.

But more than anything, she knew that she wanted him.

She rose on tiptoe, playfully bit his earlobe and whispered, "Take me home, Cameron."

Cam had never driven so fast in his entire life.

But how else was he supposed to get Elle home and out of those clothes? A speeding ticket would be well worth it.

He wasn't sure how they went from talking business to not talking at all. But when he pulled up in front of Elle's house and she bolted from the car, he realized it didn't matter in the slightest. This was what he'd been waiting for since before she'd left for DC.

He ran after her, and as soon as he'd crossed the threshold and shut the door, her mouth was on his.

"Ted," he said against her lips.

Elle shifted back, an amused expression on her face. "Calling out my dad's name while kissing me! That's definitely a first."

He grinned. "Just making sure we're alone."

"Ah. He's at his weekly poker game." Her gaze drifted to the table, where a laptop sat open, some social media site queued up. Elle tiptoed closer and read something on the screen. Her face fell.

"What is it?" Cam asked.

She threw her hand in the air. "Bayside Blogger. Again. I don't even know why I'm surprised."

Cam peered at the screen but wasn't quite sure what he was looking at.

"How does she find out this stuff so fast?" Elle met his gaze. "She reported that I'm in talks to go into business with you. Dammit!" She kicked the leg of the table.

"Calm down, Elle," he said.

"Don't tell me what to do or how to feel. You don't understand."

He held a hand up. "The Bayside Blogger saw us go into the storefront. So what?"

"I don't want my personal business broadcast around the town. Don't you understand that? Don't you know what it reminds me of?"

He softened, if only for a second. What she'd gone through in high school sucked big-time. Cam got that. But what he didn't understand was how she didn't see that experience hadn't been her fault. And how no one really cared anymore. Cam knew one thing. He didn't like seeing Elle upset. And he would do anything to ease her pain.

"You got wasted and said some nonsense on a video. Kids do a lot worse than that. Get over it."

"Stop yelling at me." She spun and headed for her room.

Cam caught up to her easily. "Stop pretending to be some wounded little victim. Guess what? You're not."

"I never said I was. It's not my fault that everyone in this town sees me as nothing more than that crazy kid who was obsessed beyond reason with Jasper."

"Then make them see. You're better than this." Cam eyed her still-unpacked suitcase in the corner of the room. A stark reminder that she could leave at any time. That sobering thought made something inside him snap. "They aren't going to stop talking about you until you shut them up. You need to address what happened back then. If you act like it's not a big deal, it won't be."

Red tinged her cheeks. She pointed at him. "You're just saying this because you don't want me to take that job in DC."

"Damn straight I don't. I want you right here."

"Well, we don't always get what we want." She crossed her arms over her chest.

Outrage looked good on her, he couldn't help thinking. "Stick up for yourself, Elle."

Her lip trembled, but only for a moment. She regained her fighting stance and jutted her chin out. "Why do you even care?"

"Because."

"Because why?" she demanded.

"Because I've gotten to know you. Because you're more than what this town thinks you are. Because you're beautiful and smart. Because you're funny and sweet and kind. Because you have passion." He closed the space between them and crushed his mouth to hers. "Because I like you."

She was panting from his kiss, and fisted her hands in the front of his shirt and drew him closer. "You like me," she stated.

"I do." He kissed her again. Hard. But then something

changed, something shifted, and Cam felt himself calming down. His lips moved over hers softly, slowly. When he lifted his head, he looked into those gorgeous green eyes. "Elle, I'm falling in love with you."

Her mouth dropped open and her eyes widened. Because he was holding her, Cam could feel her heart pounding rapidly.

When she opened her mouth to speak, Cam abruptly put a finger against her lips. "No, don't." He shook his head. "I was ready. You're not."

"But, Cam," she protested. "You just said—"

"I know what I said. It's the truth." With that, he scooped her up in his arms. She let out a little sound of pleasure at being lifted, and then pressed her lips to the side of his neck.

When he went to lay her on the bed, he paused at her giggle. "What?"

"I have a twin bed. And you're so, um…"

"What?" he repeated.

"Big."

That one word ignited something purely masculine inside him. "I'm big, huh?" With a growl, he covered her body on the small twin bed so she could feel just how big he was.

Elle let out a sigh of pleasure and simply hung on as Cam feasted on her mouth. Clinging to his shirt, she tried to keep up with him as he captured her lips, her tongue, and took and took and took.

The sensations were so heady she didn't know how long she could last like this. Nor did she know what had just happened. They'd gone from arguing to full-on making out in the blink of an eye.

But when he anchored her head with his hands and

changed the angle of the kiss, she no longer cared. All she wanted was Cam.

He said he was falling in love with her. Not only like. Love.

What was more, he hadn't needed her to say it back. He was perfectly fine to express it himself.

She loved how sure of himself and his feelings he was. She loved the way he'd challenged her tonight, both with the idea of opening a gallery and with the Bayside Blogger. She loved the way he didn't let her sulk. She loved the feel of his hands on her skin and the way his mouth roamed over hers.

Oh, my God! I love Cam.

Elle gasped and he immediately backed off her. "What's wrong?" he asked.

She looked into his brown eyes, made even darker when filled with lust. "Nothing's wrong," she told him. Because she couldn't admit that she loved him without knowing if she'd take the job in DC. It didn't seem fair to him otherwise.

She might not be ready to express her feelings out loud to him, but she could show him.

For the next few hours, that's exactly what she did.

Chapter Fifteen

I have to admit that I was quite put out to learn that Jasper Dumont, the most eligible bachelor in Bayside, had a girlfriend. However, I will forgive all of my little gossip birdies this once because I've discovered that Jasper and Mindy are on the outs. Yikes! Although, if that's the case, perhaps a new girlfriend would be the perfect present for his upcoming birthday party. Too bad Ellie Owens is already taken…

It took Cam what felt like an hour to get his breath back and his heart rate to return to normal. Each time he was with Elle, it got better and better.

Turning his head, he slanted a glance at her now. She wore a satisfied grin and nothing else. To Cam, it was the hottest ensemble he'd ever seen. He leaned over and brushed a kiss across her lips.

"You okay?" he asked.

"Mmm," she replied. She ran a hand down his side, causing him to suck in a breath. "This room is now sacred."

He met her gaze. "You mean, you've never? Here?"

Laughing, she shook her head. "Nope. I was shy in high school."

He reached for his pants and began to dress. Elle watched with an amused expression. "I see how it is. You come over here, have your way with me and disappear into the night."

"Trust me, I'd much rather stay here with you all night.

But brotherly duty calls." She raised an eyebrow. "Jasper's birthday is tomorrow. He's having a party at our parents' house. Told him I'd help set up."

"Ah." Elle rose and snagged a robe from the back of the door. As she belted the short wrap, all coherent thoughts flew out of Cam's mind. The material skimmed her thighs and the cinched belt accentuated her tiny waist. With her messy hair, flushed face, swollen lips and bare feet, she looked good enough to eat.

He made a move toward her, but Elle slapped a hand against his chest. "Oh, no, I know that look now. Come one step closer and you will definitely not make it to Jasper."

"That's okay. The kid needs to experience some disappointment now and then."

"Cam," she said with a laugh, and threw his shirt at him. "Come on, I'll walk you out."

"You did get an invite to the party, right?" he asked as he finished dressing.

"I think the entire town got an invite. Meet you there at eight?"

He nodded and they left the room. But Cam didn't want to meet her there. He wanted to come pick her up and bring her as his official date.

He wanted to hang out with her all night, talking to his friends and enjoying a beer or two. He wanted them to go back out on that gazebo where they'd spent time getting to know each other during the last party. He'd steal more kisses before returning to admire whatever over-the-top surprise his mother had planned.

He wanted to drive Elle back to his house at the end of the night and peel her out of what he was sure would be a beautiful dress. He wanted to sleep with her wrapped in his arms.

"Cam?" Elle's voice pulled him out of the dream scenario he'd just escaped to.

"Sorry." Only he wasn't sorry. Wanting to be with Elle like a normal couple wasn't some crazy, off-the-wall idea.

He pushed her up against the living room wall and took her lips in a passionate, all-consuming kiss. Eventually, Cam pulled back and muttered, "I better get going. I don't think your dad would be too thrilled to find me wrapped around his half-naked daughter."

A deep, insistent cough followed his statement, along with "You got that right."

Elle froze. Cam turned to find Ted Owens standing in the doorway, arms crossed over his chest, face beet red. He jumped back from Elle, whose face matched her father's coloring.

The robe that had seemed so sexy only a moment ago now stuck out like a flashing neon sign that read Recent Sex Romp with Your Daughter. Cam shuddered, clenched his jaw and ran a hand through his hair.

The seconds dragged. Since neither Elle nor her dad were saying anything, he tried to think of something that could break the tension. But the look on Ted's face stopped that from happening. Even though Cam probably had a good half a foot and forty pounds on Ted, he was under no presumption that the ex-cop couldn't beat the crap out of him right now if he wanted.

Everyone knew you never messed with a father when it came to his daughter.

Still, he didn't want Elle to go through what would no doubt be a very awkward conversation alone. He opened his mouth but Ted threw up a hand.

"Nope. I don't want to hear it," Ted said sternly.

"Daddy," Elle began.

"I think it's past time for Cam to leave."

Cam wasn't budging. He straightened his shoulders and reached for Elle's hand.

He caught her brief smile at the gesture.

"It's okay Cam. I got this. Really," she emphasized.

Cam swiveled his head back and forth between Elle and Ted. They wore matching resolute expressions. Had the circumstances been different, he would have laughed.

With a final squeeze to Elle's hand, he took his leave. But he felt like a coward as he went.

Elle steeled herself as the front door closed and she heard Cam's truck rev to life before heading down the street. If only she could have been so lucky.

But she wasn't, and now she was standing in the middle of unchartered waters with her father. It would really help matters if he would say something. But as of right now, he'd turned to stone, holding his position of "pissed-off daddy" while nailing her with a rigid stare.

Could he just say something? Begin the conversation? It would almost be better if he started yelling. But this silent treatment was beyond uncomfortable. Where did parents learn that, anyway?

"Daddy," she finally murmured.

Ted held up a hand. "Are you and Cameron dating?"

She made sure her robe was still securely belted. "Well, we're, um…"

"Because the only reason to find your daughter looking like that—" he pointed at her "—and coming out of there with a man—" he gestured toward her bedroom "—is if she is in a serious, committed, monogamous relationship." He cocked an eyebrow and waited.

Elle sank into the nearest chair. "It's complicated."

Ted nodded. His cheeks were still red, but she could tell the fight had gone out of him. He walked to the kitchen, came back with his favorite whiskey and poured a glass for each of them. Then he downed his in about half a second.

"It's complicated?" He repeated her words. "Let's un-complicate it."

Elle wanted nothing more. But first, she needed to change into something that was a little less revealing. She ran to her room and threw on a pair of yoga pants and a sweatshirt. Then she returned to the living room and tossed back her shot of whiskey, the fiery liquid coating her throat and causing her to cough. "I can't talk to you about this."

"Why not? I'm your father."

Elle held on to her glass, turning it around and around. "That's kind of why I can't."

"Well, I don't see a line of people ready to listen. Looks like right now I'm all you got."

Something softened in Elle's heart. She took in her father, the first man to ever love her. "You've always been all I've got."

"Come here, princess."

She joined him on the couch.

"Tell me what's going on."

So she did. He already knew about her interview and job offer in DC, but Elle filled him in on Cam's idea for the gallery.

Ted appeared to be deep in thought. "Your options are to either take a job that you are well qualified for and you would probably love, in a city that is exciting and interesting and not too far from here."

"Right," she said.

"Or you can take a huge risk and do something new. Something that you would probably be good at, but will take a lot of hard work and would be very scary. And would have you staying in Bayside."

Again, she nodded. Then she gnawed on her lip and looked away.

"There's more, isn't there?" her dad asked.

Elle took a deep breath. "The Bayside Blogger has already reported that I had an interview and that Cam showed me the property for the gallery."

Her dad narrowed his eyes. "What in the hell does that Blogger have to do with any of this? More important, what does it have to do with deciding between the job in DC and opening a gallery here—which, by the way, I think you should do."

She wanted to scream. Her dad wanted her to stay in Bayside?

"Ellie?" He looked at her imploringly.

"Every time I see my name on that damn blog or in her column or on her Twitter account, I get this feeling in my stomach."

Concern filled his eyes. "But why, sweetheart?"

With a deep, shuddering breath, Elle let it all out. "Because I'm so worried that I embarrass you. That every time something about me goes public, you are humiliated, just like you were back when I was in high school." She stalked to the window. "I want to stay here, Daddy. I want to open a gallery. But I'm afraid that you don't want me to be here." She turned to look at him.

Elle didn't think it was possible, but her dad's face turned even redder than when he'd caught her and Cam together. Only this time he was angry.

"Don't want you here? Of course I want you here. Do you have any idea how much I've missed you these past ten years?"

"But you always encouraged me to stay in Italy."

"Because you love art. You always have. Where else were you going to get experience like that? I wanted the best for my child. That's what good parents do."

Elle sank into the soft cushions, feeling completely depleted. "But you sent me away to college. After, well, you know, after that thing in high school."

Ted nodded. "Ellie, you had already been accepted to that school. I suggested you do the prefreshman courses because I saw how embarrassed you were over that video. I thought it would be good for you to get away. You thought I sent you away?" He lowered his gaze. "If you'd spoken up and told me you didn't want to go, I would have never pressed the issue."

"But weren't you mad about that video?"

His gaze snapped up to meet hers. "Of course I was mad. Those girls got you drunk and filmed you."

A strangled sound escaped her throat. "You knew? All this time you knew it wasn't my fault?"

"Of course I knew. You were a good girl, Ellie. Why, all of sudden and right before you were set to graduate, would you decide to rebel? It didn't make sense. I knew you'd had a sleepover with those girls. You didn't get in more trouble at school because I spoke to that idiot principal."

"You did?"

"I also spoke to the parents of those girls. Unfortunately, I didn't have any concrete proof. As a cop, I understood I could only take the issue so far."

"You stuck up for me?"

Ted grabbed her hand and squeezed hard. "Always."

"But I thought that video contributed to you losing the county sheriff election."

Ted shrugged. "Maybe. But there was more to that election than one little teenage prank. There was a group of men who didn't want me as sheriff. I knew some of them were doing some shady things. I'll spare you the details," he said, in response to Elle's questioning gaze. "Look, honey. I might've lost, but I still had a good, long career that I'm proud of."

Elle sat back against the cushions and let out the longest breath she'd ever held. In fact, she may have been keeping it in for the last ten years. All this time she'd carried around guilt and shame. And now her dad was telling her that she'd misinterpreted everything? She would laugh if she wasn't feeling so exhausted.

"Wait a minute." Elle realized something. "At the spring festival, when they were doing that awful stunt at the water, I saw you in the crowd. You turned away from me."

Her dad appeared truly confused. "Was I wearing my glasses that day?"

Elle couldn't remember. More than likely, he wasn't. Ted forgot his glasses more than anyone she knew. "I guess you weren't."

Ted deflated. "The truth is, I did see you that day. And I saw what that moron Chumsky was doing. I was about to lose my mind when Ernie and the guys called me back."

"What?" Elle asked, shocked.

"I had a mind to slash that fool's car tires."

Elle's mouth dropped open. "Daddy!"

Ted shrugged. "Don't worry, I didn't do it. But no one's going to mess with my baby." He leaned over and cuddled her against him for a long-overdue hug. Then he kissed the top of her head and said the words she'd needed to hear for years. "The truth is, I want nothing more than for you to come live in Bayside again."

Her eyes filled and she hiccuped, trying to hold the tears at bay.

"Shh, none of that." He shifted, reaching in his pocket for his cloth handkerchief. "Now that that's all settled, let's get back to discussing this complicated thing with Cam."

Elle groaned. "I think I preferred talking about my adolescent traumas."

"I could tell that boy had a thing for you from the moment you got home. And he'd be a damn fool not to act on it now."

"He's not a fool. But I think I've been one. I'm the one who needs to act on it."

Ted kissed her head again. "Then get to it. Now that you're staying in Bayside, a couple grandkids would suit me just fine."

She would have rolled her eyes, but after their conversation Elle felt happier and lighter than she had in forever. All she wanted to do tonight was sit with her father, knowing she was going to be sitting with him for a long, long time.

Chapter Sixteen

New couple alert. I have definitive proof that Ellie Owens and Cam Dumont have apparently been getting it on. Look for their debut at Jasper's birthday party tonight!

Elle climbed the steps of the Dumont estate promptly at eight o'clock. She was ushered inside by a maid and shown to the solarium.

There was a spring in her step that had nothing to do with the semi-uncomfortable, yet utterly fabulous sparkly heels she wore. Her good mood could mostly be attributed to her conversation with her dad the night before. The two-ton brick of emotions that had been weighing her down for ten years was gone and Elle finally felt at peace.

Well, almost, she reminded herself. She still needed to tell Cam that she'd made her decision. She'd called the Smithsonian that morning and declined the job offer. Elle was going to buy that space in town and open a gallery, and she couldn't wait to see Cam's face when she told him.

Entering the solarium, she noticed that tonight's gathering was a much more intimate get-together than the *Printemps* party. She saw Mr. and Mrs. Dumont and a few older people that Elle assumed worked with Jasper. For the most part, though, the crowd consisted of people her age—former classmates and others she'd seen around town.

The decorations were sparse but tasteful. The solarium was a beautiful room with large glass windows and French doors that opened up to one of the terraces. People spilled outside, laughter and music mingling with the scent of yummy food. Elle turned as a waiter passed by with a tray.

"Pancetta-wrapped scallop?" he offered.

She smiled and popped one of the appetizers into her mouth.

She spotted Riley, who was in deep conversation with her boss, Sawyer Wallace. It looked pretty intense, so Elle walked to one of the many bars set up around the room and ordered a glass of champagne.

Riley and Sawyer eventually made their way over and ordered drinks. Riley gave Elle a quick hug. "Love the dress, Elle," she said with a wink.

Riley had picked out the short lilac number while they were in DC. Elle indulged her by doing a little spin.

"I smell a shopping enabler," Sawyer said. "Riley has ruined many a friend's credit rating."

"Oh, aren't you just hysterical. Ha, ha, ha." Riley rolled her eyes.

Sawyer was incredibly good-looking, Elle thought. He was tall, with blondish-brown hair that might be a couple weeks past due for a cut. Not to mention he had an adorable smile and hazel eyes that appeared to twinkle right now as if he was in on some kind of joke.

Elle smiled and stuck out her hand. "I'm Elle Owens. We haven't officially met yet."

"Sawyer Wallace." He returned her smile and shook her hand. "Nice to officially meet you. Although, between Riley's daily recaps of your exploits and the Bayside Blogger's columns, I feel like I know you."

At first Elle gritted her teeth at the mention of the Bayside Blogger. But suddenly, she pointed a finger at Sawyer. "Wait a minute. You know who this Blogger is. Why don't you tell me?"

Sawyer made a gesture like he was locking his lips. "I wish I could, but I've made a solemn vow."

"And he won't break it for anyone," Riley added. "Don't bother, Elle. I've tried."

But Elle was undeterred. "What do I have to give you? Money? A new car?"

Sawyer laughed and took a long swig of his beer. "Trust me, you are not the first to make me such offers. And you probably won't be the last. The truth is, I get more revenue from advertisers who specifically request to be in her section in the paper or on her page on the website than any other place."

Elle sighed. "She's your bread and butter right now."

"Just a bit." Sawyer must have noticed someone come in because he gave a little nod toward the entryway. "Cam's here. I'm gonna go say hi. Oh, and congrats, Elle. I think you and Cam make a really nice couple."

She blinked. "What did he just say?" she whispered to Riley, as Sawyer crossed the room and slapped a hand on Cam's back.

Riley turned her away from the crowd. "Um, I didn't want to say anything, but…"

Elle's eyes rolled back so far they were practically on the second floor. "Let me guess how this sentence is going to end. You're going to ask me if I've seen the Bayside Blogger's column today, aren't you?"

Riley looked sheepish as she nodded.

"Give it to me straight. What did she say?"

But before Riley could fill her in, Elle heard a couple standing nearby talking rather loudly.

"Ellie Owens and Cam Dumont are together. Like, together-together. As a couple."

"I think it's awful. What about Jasper? Ellie just led him on."

"Whatever! I'd take either of those brothers in a heartbeat."

Elle's stomach sank.

Riley leaned closer. "She said you and Cam were in a relationship now."

Oh, God. Elle peeked around the room. Cam was making his way toward her, a big grin on his face. At the same time, hushed whispers and curious glances occurred all around her.

"Great. Just great," she muttered.

Riley rubbed Elle's arm. "I'm sorry, Elle. I'll let you and Cam talk."

Elle thanked her friend and greeted Cam with a scowl.

"Hey, gorgeous," he said, oblivious to the latest gossip.

"Shh," she urged. Then she snatched his hand and pulled him to the far side of the room and a quiet, dark corner.

"What? What's going on?" he asked, eyes darting around the room.

"The Bayside Blogger outed us."

Cam appeared stricken. "She said we were gay?"

Elle rolled her eyes. "No. She said we were dating. That we're together. In a relationship."

Elle waited, but Cam didn't respond. Understanding flooded his face, only to be replaced by a red blush that covered his neck, his cheeks and even the tips of his ears. But he wasn't embarrassed, she quickly realized. He was angry.

He grabbed her arm. "Dammit, Elle. We *are* in a relationship."

Her pulse picked up. "That's not what I meant."

"Yes, it is." He ran a hand over his face and then let that hand fall in frustration. "I can't do this anymore."

Pure, unadulterated panic washed over her. Her throat was tight as she asked, "Can't do what?"

He gestured between them. "This. That." He pointed to the rest of the room. "I'm glad the Bayside Blogger put that in her column. I don't want to keep us quiet anymore. Hell, I should have thought to tip her off myself."

His voice had grown louder and quite a few heads turned in their direction. But Cam didn't seem to notice or care. Instead, he pulled her close to him. "I want to be with you in front of these people. I want to kiss you. But I'll tell you what I don't want to do—what I'm not going to do anymore. Hide."

He released her and abruptly turned his back. As he made his way through the room, an icy feeling spread throughout her body. She couldn't let him leave like this.

Running after him, she called out, "Cam, please wait." Then she reached for his arm, but he shrugged her off.

They were in the middle of the room. Cam shook his head. "I'm done waiting." After a last long look at her, one filled with regret, he fled the party.

Tears welled up in Elle's eyes, but she did her best to keep them from spilling over. Her cheeks were hot and she was aware that the music had stopped and everyone was openly staring at her.

"Elle?" She felt a hand on her back and turned to find Jasper's kind eyes. "What happened? Where did Cam go?"

"I, um, I think he left. I think I really messed up." She pointed to the door and then back to Jasper.

"Ooh, look! Now Ellie and Jasper are together."

"Wait. Which one is she into?"

"Did Ellie and Cam just break up?"

"Were they together? I thought she was in love with Jasper."

The whispers and questions poured in, and that's when she realized that she'd totally and irrevocably erred. She'd treated Cam like some dirty little secret, when in reality he was the best thing that had ever happened to her.

She'd pushed him away because she was so afraid people would gossip about her. Elle glanced around the room. That was happening, anyway. And now Cam wasn't by her side.

She stepped back from Jasper and fought the urge to start biting her nails. Her heart hurt.

Her gaze whizzed around the room, from one decked-out partygoer to the next. Who was this damn Blogger and why was she so intent on making a mockery of Elle's life?

Cam had been right. She needed to put a stop to this now. Right this very minute. The Elle Show had to come to an end.

She grabbed a champagne flute and a knife from a nearby table. When she clinked the knife against the glass, the room slowly quieted down and everyone turned in her direction.

Elle experienced a brief moment of terror at having so many people look at her at the same time. But then she remembered the *Printemps* party, and how she'd gotten through it. Because of Cam. Cam, who she'd just massively pissed off.

"Are you giving a toast?" someone in the crowd called out.

"Yes. Sort of," she said, her voice wavering. "I have a few things to clear up." She projected so everyone in the solarium could hear her. Her palms began to sweat when she noticed that people were even making their way inside from the terrace to listen.

She saw Jasper move forward on her left side. Riley and Sawyer were standing in the middle of the room, a curious expression on both their faces. Mr. and Mrs. Dumont were watching from their seats at one of the high tables near the French doors.

"Are you going to sing 'Happy Birthday'?" someone else asked.

"No. But happy birthday, Jasper. Thanks for having us," she said lamely. She cleared her throat one more time. "I know I was the star of a really bad video in high school, where I declared my love for the birthday boy."

"And then you jumped in the bay."

"Thank you, Tony," she called out, making a mental note not to tip him the next time she went to The Brewside.

"That video wasn't my fault. A couple girls spiked my drinks at a sleepover. I had no idea they did that, or that I was being filmed that night." A shocked murmur filtered through the crowd. She even thought she heard a *poor Ellie*.

Continuing, Elle said, "I didn't throw myself in the bay back in high school. Or last month. I simply slipped. Both times."

Since she was holding a glass filled with alcohol, and she wasn't much for public speaking to begin with, she downed the drink, the bubbles filling her with liquid courage.

"I stayed away from Bayside for ten years because of that video." A collective gasp roared through the crowd. "But you know what? I'm not running away again. This is my home, and I'm back to stay."

A couple claps were mixed with calls of *good for you* and *awesome*.

"And furthermore, I'm in love with Cam Dumont." Gasps, sighs and a loud whoop sounded throughout the room at this revelation. "Only I may have messed it up pretty bad."

She sighed. "Except for my dad, Cam is the greatest man I've ever known. Cam was the only person who really listened to me when I first got back. He's honorable and hardworking. He started his own company without any help or support."

Elle thought she spotted Cam's parents sit up straighter at that comment. They definitely exchanged a glance. She met Jasper's gaze. "And he worries about his brother all the time."

Jasper cocked his head, his formerly amused expression morphing into confusion.

It occurred to her that she probably shouldn't be revealing so much about other people, but she couldn't seem to stop. She veered back to herself.

"So that's what I have to say." She nodded firmly.

"Well done, Ellie," someone called from the back of the room.

She held up a finger. "Okay, one more thing." A few laughs rang out. "My name is Elle, not Ellie. Ellie is a little girl's name and I am a grown, accomplished woman. So, from now on, I'm Elle Owens, daughter of Ted Owens. I'm hopefully opening an art gallery down near the water. If you'll excuse me, I have to go."

With that, Elle turned toward the exit with her head held high. Applause and cheers followed her out the door as she went to track down the man she loved.

Chapter Seventeen

Ugh... Even bloggers get hung over after big soirees. What was your favorite part of Jasper's party? I think a certain speech made by our town's own prodigal daughter takes the cake. Don't believe me? Check out the best video I've taken in a while...

And PS. I think it's time we all start calling her Elle.

Cam was brooding. Full-on feeling sorry for himself, considering drinking himself into a stupor, forget this damn day and anything that had to do with Elle Owens brooding.

He stalked from the living room to his kitchen. He opened the fridge, grabbed a beer, then put it back on the shelf and slammed the door.

Restless, irritable and tired as hell, Cam contemplated going for a run, doing a little boxing at the gym, cutting some wood or just blasting hard rock.

In the end, he went for the music.

The only problem was that the heavy bass exacerbated the headache he had from not sleeping well. He sank into his favorite leather recliner. But the chair did nothing to soothe his mood. Or calm his nerves.

Because what he really needed to do was turn off his brain. The brain that was running a loop of Elle at the party last night. Elle refusing to admit they were in a relationship. Elle once again declining to stand up for herself.

And that's what really got to him. If she'd only tell everyone what was what, they'd probably back off, leave her alone. Because once she could be honest, there'd be nothing to gossip about.

And yeah, he wouldn't have minded being acknowledged as her boyfriend. Or at least someone she was sleeping with.

Still, as angry as he was today, he wondered how she was doing. He couldn't help but worry over what might have happened after he made his getaway. Cam knew he'd do just about anything for her.

Except pretend. He no longer would—or could—pretend there wasn't something between them. He loved her.

Then, without warning, his loud music stopped. The hard guitar riffs and pounding beat of the drums ended.

Cam looked over at his stereo and saw his brother standing there, watching him with his arms crossed over his chest. "What's the matter?" Jasper asked.

Cam shrugged. "I don't know." But he did know. He raked a hand through his hair and the floodgate simply collapsed. "I'm in love with someone and she can't even muster up the courage to admit we're dating. I guess I don't know her as well as I thought."

To Cam's amazement, Jasper grinned.

"What in the hell is so funny?"

"You are a clueless Neanderthal."

Cam could feel his headache returning even stronger. He pinned his brother with a hard stare.

"Hold on. Let me explain," Jasper said quickly.

Cam went to the kitchen and returned with two bottles of beer. "Here. Drink. Talk."

Jasper made himself comfortable in one of Cam's chairs. After a long swig of beer, Jasper met Cam's gaze. "You're in love with her."

"I already told you that."

Jasper let out a big sigh. The kind of sigh you give to a kid who says something stupid and you're trying to remain patient. "I noticed how you were around her the first time I saw Elle. Remember that day in the town square? I didn't recognize her at first. You had it bad back then."

Rising from the chair, Jasper walked around the room. "But I had no idea exactly how bad until I saw your face last night. It really hurt you when she didn't acknowledge you were in a relationship."

"Again, I've already stated this. Do you have a point?"

Jasper grinned, but the smile didn't reach his eyes. "Several. First off, don't give up on Elle. Seriously."

Cam downed the rest of his beer and considered grabbing another one. "After last night, I don't think there is anything to go back to. I won't pretend."

"Okay, let's table the Elle situation for a moment. There's something else."

"There always is," Cam groaned.

"Elle said something after you left last night." Jasper shook his head. "It…surprised me."

"What did she say?" Curious, Cam sat back and waited.

Jasper didn't speak at first. He seemed to be having an internal debate before he finally looked at Cam. "Are you worried about me?"

Of course. But Cam couldn't bring himself to say that out loud. "You're my brother," he said instead.

Jasper got up and stood right in front of Cam, crowding his space. "I'm going to ask you something and I want you to be brutally honest with me. Seriously," he added, when Cam shifted in his seat. "Do not lie or try to protect me or do whatever it is you big brothers do."

"Okay, fine."

"When I took over your spot in Mom and Dad's company," he began. But then he paused. "You've said some things in the past. Do you think I'm unhappy working there?"

Cam moved to get up, but Jasper blocked him. He settled for staring out the window and running a hand over the stubble on his chin.

"Come on, Cam," Jasper urged.

Too exhausted to fight or even to lie, Cam finally let it out. "The guilt I feel…"

"Guilt? Guilt over what?" Jasper asked.

"I made you take the job at our parents' company."

Jasper backed up. "No, you didn't."

"I mean, I didn't force you, but if it hadn't been for me, you wouldn't have stepped up. And you and Dad are at each other's throats all the time."

"That's because Dad can be really stubborn. So can Mom when it comes to it."

"I love my business and my job. But I feel guilty every single day." Cam sighed when Jasper cocked his head. He was going to have to spell this out for him. "If I hadn't been selfish and quit, you wouldn't have had to stand in for me."

Silence filled the room for a full minute. Then Jasper sat next to Cam on the couch. "Do you know what it was like to be born second in this family? To be the younger son?"

Cam shook his head.

"It sucks." His brother scrubbed a hand over his face. "Every single thing I ever did was discounted. Didn't matter."

"That's not true." Loyalty swelled in Cam for his little brother.

"Afraid it is. You were the one who mattered. You were the coveted heir, the future of the company. I was the spare."

Jesus. Was that how it had really been? "Don't ever say that again. You know you were loved."

"I do. But I wasn't respected." He stood up once more and began to pace. "I love real estate. I love crunching numbers. I love making deals. I love coming up with new ideas to expand the business. I love all of it."

"You do?"

"Yes. I always have. Why do you think I spent so much time following Dad around when I was little? Why do you think I spend so much time talking with Mom now? I worked my butt off to get into great schools and prepare myself for a place in the family business. When you told me you didn't want to work for Mom and Dad, secretly I was thrilled."

"I'll be damned."

"I'm sorry to say this, Cam, but I'm the one who's a selfish bastard. I didn't step in to help you out of a jam. I stepped in because I was finally getting exactly what I wanted."

Cam walked over to his brother. "Are you serious?"

"Yep." Jasper nodded firmly. "So you don't owe me anything."

Overwhelmed with emotion and feeling lighter than he had in years, Cam did something he hadn't done since they'd been young. He grabbed his little brother in a tight bear hug.

"Thanks, you little snot."

"Anytime, bro." Jasper pushed away. "Now, back to Elle. You gonna go after her or what?"

Exhaling a long, frustrated sigh of breath, Cam sank back onto the couch.

"You haven't visited the Bayside Blogger's column today, have you?" Jasper asked.

Cam rolled his eyes. "Oh, yeah, I checked it out right after I did some online shopping and watched a chick flick."

"Look, I know you're not a fan. But if there's one day for you to make an exception, today really should be that day."

"Why? Is she talking about who wore what to your party last night?"

Jasper chuckled. "Oh, she's definitely talking about my

party." After reaching into his pocket, he threw his phone over to Cam. "Pull it up. There's a video blog today."

"I really don't care about—"

"Watch the freaking thing already," Jasper said, impatience dripping from his voice.

Fine, Cam thought. When Jasper wanted something, he was like a dog with a bone. Even though he was in no mood to watch—what? Probably two people making out at the party, or someone wearing the wrong kind of outfit. But since he was having a moment with his brother, he figured he'd go for it.

Pulling up the website on Jasper's phone, Cam felt his heart drop when an image of Elle in her purple dress filled the screen. He pressed Play on the video clip and also saw Jasper, and could tell they were talking, but he couldn't hear anything.

"Turn up the volume, Einstein."

Offering his brother a finger of choice, he increased the volume and sat back to watch Elle Owens, the woman he was in love with, go nuts on the entire town. By the end of the video, his heart had stopped and he hadn't taken a breath.

He flicked hopeful eyes up to Jasper.

"She loves me"

His brother merely nodded.

Cam threw the phone back at him and jumped off the couch. "I gotta go."

"About time," Jasper called, as Cam ran in search of his keys. He had to find Elle.

He heard Jasper settle on the couch and flip on the television as he headed for the door. Cam burst through it and almost ran smack-dab into his father.

"Dad," he said, surprised. "What are you doing here?"

Collin Dumont was an older, more mature version of Cam. They were the same height, had the same dark looks and tanned skin. The only difference besides their choice of occupations was that Collin could nail his sons with the most intense fatherly stare. From the time Cam had been a little kid, one look from his dad and he would stop in his tracks.

At thirty-two, the same could still be said.

"I need a minute," his dad said, walking to the railing of the porch Cam had built himself. Collin stroked the finished wood and gave an appreciative nod. "This is good work."

Cam stayed quiet.

"This your work?" he asked.

Cam nodded and joined him at the railing. "Yep. The place didn't come with a porch, and with a setup like this, it was screaming for one."

Collin leaned back and seemed to take in the small Cape Cod house that Cam loved.

Leaning a hip against the railing, Cam tried to clamp down on the urge to brush his dad off. He desperately wanted to find Elle.

"I wanted to tell you something." Collin said. "Elle stated a lot of things last night. That's why I'm here."

When Elle finally decided to speak up, she really let loose, Cam thought with a grin.

"You do good work, Cam."

Surprised, Cam blinked. "Um, thanks."

"I don't tell you enough." Collin gave a short chuckle. "I don't tell you ever."

"I noticed," he replied.

"I wanted you to take over the company the same way I had from my father."

"Dad," Cam began, hearing the angst in his voice. "We've discussed this to death."

His father held up a hand. "I was stubborn about it. Perhaps too stubborn."

Cam shot him a look. A very surprised look.

To his credit, Collin appeared ruffled. He ran his hand through his hair the same way Cam often did. "You are your own man. You started a successful business without any help from me." His voice broke as he said, "I'm so proud of you, son."

Around a very tight throat, Cam replied, "Thanks, Dad."

Not one for overly emotional scenes, Collin slapped a hand on his back. "Very proud. I need to come look at some of your work soon. Not every man has such a talented son."

"You actually have two talented sons." Cam nodded toward his house, where Jasper had no doubt found one of the many movie channels Cam subscribed to.

Collin peered inside, as well. "I know."

"Wouldn't hurt you to tell him from time to time," Cam suggested.

"I know that, too. His time will come. Jasper still has a little more to learn."

Cam figured this would probably be the biggest Hallmark moment he ever had with his dad. But he still wanted to get to Elle.

"Where were you running off to when I interrupted?" Collin asked quite perceptively.

"Actually, I have to go talk to someone."

"Is someone a very attractive brunette who caused quite a stir last night?" He offered a rare grin.

"Seems like it. Not sure how you're going to feel about this," Cam said, as he walked down the porch steps. "I'm about to do something kind of risky."

"All good businessmen take risks," Collin said.

"I'm in love with Elle Owens and I'm going to try and win her back."

Collin crossed his arms over his chest and gave him a

steady, yet supportive, stare. "Well, if one of you didn't go after her, I would have thought I'd raised two idiots."

Elle had been all over Bayside. Her feet were sore, her head was pounding and she was exhausted.

She'd begun her day with her dad, who let her accompany him to his doctor's appointment. Even though she'd barely slept and wanted to talk to Cam immediately, she couldn't be happier that her dad was finally letting her in, so she'd tabled her get-Cam-back plans.

After the doctor's visit, she'd had to postpone finding Cam again, for another good reason. She'd visited the bank, spending hours going over paperwork and interest rates and preapprovals. Just thinking of it made her head swim. Although not as much as the fact that she was going to be a business owner.

Elle smiled. If all went well, she was going to be the owner of Bayside Gallery. She still couldn't believe it. She was going to stay in her hometown and be close to her dad.

And close to Cam. Who currently hated her.

She let out a long, frustrated sigh. She'd been everywhere looking for him, even his parents' house. She'd left no less than twenty messages on his cell phone. But he hadn't answered and he wasn't in any of the usual places she thought she'd find him. Not at The Brewside or Max's. His house had been empty, except for Jasper, who'd made himself comfortable with a big bowl of popcorn and Cam's big-screen TV. He'd been no help, though, just grinning at her like a loon.

Her next step was to drive down to Cam's cabin. But first she needed a moment.

Looking out at the bay, she took in the serene water, so calm today. So different from how she was feeling.

Why hadn't she taken his hand last night? She wanted him. She…loved him.

Instead, he'd run out and she'd completely lost her mind. Although he may have been on to something with the whole sticking-up-for-yourself bit. Perhaps it was all in her mind, but people were acting differently toward her today.

And Elle liked it.

With a final exhalation that did nothing to relax her, she stood, smoothed down her bright orange blouse—a Riley selection—and turned back toward the street. That's when she froze.

Cam.

There he was, running toward her. As if she'd wished him into existence.

"Elle," he called. In a few long strides he was at her side.

"Cam!" She released a long breath. "I've been looking for you all day. I'm so sorry about last night. You have no idea." The words rushed out of her. It felt like if she didn't get them all out immediately, she would burst.

"I've been so stupid," she continued. Cam opened his mouth, but she shook her head and put a finger to his lips. "No, you were right. You were so right about everything."

She shoved her hands into the pockets of her jeans and bit her lip. She had to go on. "You were right about sticking up for myself, and I finally did after you left last night."

He shifted and she could tell he was going to try and say something, so she kept going. "I had a long talk with my dad the other night. I've been an idiot with him, too. He's so happy I'm going to stay in Bayside."

Cam lifted an eyebrow and she laughed. "Yes, I'm staying. Depending on my preapproval, I'm going to open the gallery. Of course, I'll still do nursery murals and other side jobs, too."

His face softened and that was exactly what she needed to see. "Thank you," she said with a long sigh.

Cam grinned. "What are you thanking me for?"

"Thank you for believing in me. Thank you for not

judging me." She took a step toward him. "Thank you for pushing me." She gave him a little shove for emphasis. "Thank you for being my friend." Clutching his hands, she met his eyes. "Thank you for being more than my friend."

"Anything else?" he asked.

She nodded. "Most important, thank you for calling me Elle."

He laughed and pulled her to him for a long, overdue embrace. Their lips met and she melted. Elle didn't know how long they stayed like that and she didn't care. The only thing that mattered was that they were together.

Cam lifted his head. "That was a lot to confess," he said.

"There's one more thing I have to tell you."

"Oh, yeah? I'm intrigued."

She framed his face with her hands. "I love you, Cam Dumont."

He growled and crushed his mouth to hers. But the kiss quickly went from passionate to sweet and ended with Cam kissing the tip of her nose. "I watched the video of your speech on the Bayside Blogger's site. I'm so proud of you, Elle. I love you, too."

"So kiss me again and prove it."

He did just that, walking her backward until she felt the railing against her legs. All of a sudden, a creaking noise rang out and next thing Elle knew, she could no longer feel the railing on her skin. She didn't feel anything except that heady sensation of free-falling.

And with a big splash, they both went into the bay.

Yet again.

When she surfaced, Cam grabbed her. They stared at each other as they treaded water. After a moment, they burst into laughter.

"What is it with you and this water?"

"I just can't get enough."

"And I can't get enough of you." He kissed her again.

Funny, Elle thought. Everything seemed to have started with a video and her falling into the bay that night in high school. She looked at Cam. "You really watched the Bayside Blogger's video?"

"Yep. That damn gossip may have just saved us."

"Too bad she wasn't around a couple minutes ago. Maybe she could have saved us from falling in. I thought you fixed the railing?"

"I must have missed a portion. I'll have to come back tomorrow."

"With me. We'll fix it together."

As the sun began to set over their heads and water lapped around them, Elle wrapped her arms around Cam and kissed him. Perfectly content with her life and her man, all thanks to the meddling of a certain blogger.

Epilogue

Smiling, the Bayside Blogger powered off her laptop and flipped the lid closed. She did love a happy ending.

Rising from the table in The Brewside, she sneaked a glance around the room. As always, everyone was oblivious to her identity. Just as she liked it.

She knew her blog had upset people initially, but in the end, they had to realize she was only reporting the truth. And if you stuck to the truth, no one could really say anything bad. Her mother always said she had a talent for reading people and their emotions. Of course, her mother had wanted her to go into psychology or some other prestigious field. But she was happy right where she was.

She pretended not to be interested as people poured into the coffee shop, gossiping about Elle Owens and Cam Dumont falling into the bay. Again.

"I tried to give them a hand, help them out," someone was saying. "But they just kept making out."

She laughed along with everyone else. If she was alone, she'd pat herself on the back. In her mind, she'd definitely helped Elle and Cam along. Sometimes people just needed a little push.

But secretly, what she really wanted was a happy ending of her own. Maybe someday soon, she'd find that special person…

Until then, she had a feeling someone else needed her attention. As if conjured from her thoughts, Jasper Dumont strode into The Brewside. He greeted a couple friends and chuckled at the story of his brother and Elle.

Yes, Jasper needed some help. She was sure of it. And then maybe, perhaps, after that, she could take some time to find her own happiness.

Shaking her head, she reminded herself that just by giving them a few mentions here and there, she'd given Elle and Cam their happy ending. For now, that would have to be enough.

"Bye, Tony," she called with a friendly wave.

Her work here was done. Two more people saved by the blog.

* * * * *

Don't miss Jasper Dumont's story,
The next installment in SAVED BY THE BLOG,
Kerri Carpenter's new miniseries for
Harlequin Special Edition

Coming soon!

#2557 THE MAVERICK FAKES A BRIDE!
Montana Mavericks: The Great Family Roundup
by Christine Rimmer
Travis Dalton needs a fake fiancée fast, or he'll be cut from the final cast of a cowboy reality show. Bold, adventurous Brenna O'Reilly is perfect for the role. Too bad pretending they're lovers for the cameras quickly has Travis and Brenna wishing this game of love would never have to end.

#2558 A SECOND CHANCE FOR THE SINGLE DAD
Matchmaking Mamas • by Marie Ferrarella
Dr. Luke Dolan is a recently widowed, floundering single dad who also happens to need a nurse for his new practice. Lucky for him, the Matchmaking Mamas know just who to call! Kayley Quartermain is a nurse looking for direction and perhaps a happy ending of her very own...

#2559 SAY YES TO THE COWBOY
Thunder Mountain Brotherhood • by Vicki Lewis Thompson
Tess Irwin is elated to find herself pregnant, though not so much about the fact that Zeke Rafferty is the father. But the former foster child can't turn his back on his child. Can they work out a visitation compromise without getting their hearts broken in the process?

#2560 A BRIDE, A BARN, AND A BABY
Celebration, TX • by Nancy Robards Thompson
Lucy Campbell is thrilled Zane Phillips finally sees her as more than his friend's little sister. Until she gets pregnant! Refusing to trap him into marriage, she rejects his proposal. But Zane is beginning to realize he just might want everything Lucy has to offer after all.

#2561 IT STARTED WITH A DIAMOND
Drake Diamonds • by Teri Wilson
When Diana Drake, a diamond heiress, and Franco Andrade, a disgraced polo player, pretend to be engaged for their own selfish reasons, their charade soon becomes more real than either of them intended.

#2562 HOME TO WICKHAM FALLS
Wickham Falls Weddings • by Rochelle Alers
Sawyer Middleton swore he would never return to his hometown, but when a family emergency forces his hand, he meets Jessica Calhoun, an intriguing teacher who has *forever* written all over her. Will this free-wheeling city boy give up his fast-paced life in the face of love?

HSECNM0617

SPECIAL EXCERPT FROM

HQN™

*A rising-star art investigator finds herself captivated
by Icon, an enigmatic international art thief whose
heists are methodical, daring, baffling. To Zara the
case is maddening—bordering on an obsession. She
finds distraction in the arms of a magnetic American
billionaire but, as she surrenders to his captivating allure
and glamorous world, she must determine if it's the real
thing…or just a convincing forgery.*

*Enjoy a sneak peek of
THE CHASE, the first book in the **ICON** series
by USA TODAY bestselling author Vanessa Fewings.*

My gaze fixed on the living, breathing sculpture.

My heartbeat quickened as I searched my memory for
where I knew him from. I was awestruck by this breathtaking
Adonis, who was reaching for a white shirt hanging on the
back of a chair. He was tall and devastatingly handsome
in a rugged kind of way. Thirty, maybe? Those short, dark
golden locks framing a gorgeous face, his three-day stubble
marking him with a tenacious edge and that thin wry smile
exuding a fierce confidence. His intense, steady glare stayed
on mine as he calmly pulled his arm through a sleeve and
covered that tattoo before I could make out more.

A gasp caught in my throat as it came to me that we'd
never actually met, probably because this was Tobias
William Wilder, a billionaire. He moved in the kind of
refined circles one would expect from a business magnate
and inventor who owned TechRule, one of the largest
software companies in the world.

And I'd given this playboy mogul his very own peep
show.

I'd read an article on him, featuring his Los Angeles–based art gallery, The Wilder. It was an acclaimed museum that was one of the most prestigious in the world.

Although I'd imagined one day I might bump into him with the art world being relatively small, never had I imagined a scenario as racy as this.

"I'm looking for the stairs," I managed.

"That way." His refined American accent felt like another blow to my reason.

That alpha-maleness made him look like he'd just returned from a dangerous adventure in the Himalayas or even the jungles of Peru…

A waft of expensive musky cologne reached me with its sensuous allure and did something crazy to my body.

"You might want to put some clothes on," I said firmly.

"Well, now I'm dressed."

Yes, he was, and this was a changing room, apparently, and I'd not exactly represented a pillar of virtue.

"Well that's good." I swallowed my pride. "Please keep it that way."

His gaze lowered to my feet.

And I remembered my strappy stilettos were flirtatiously dangling from my left hand, those spiked heels hinting at a sexy side I wished I had.

Intrigue marred his face, and then his expression softened again as his jade gaze returned to hold mine.

I left in a rush, shaken with just how this man had affected me merely with a smile.

I felt an inexplicable need to run back in and continue to bathe in the aura of the most enigmatic man I'd ever met.

Will Zara risk it all when she finds herself on a collision course with danger and desire?

Find out when THE CHASE by USA TODAY bestselling author Vanessa Fewings goes on sale in June 2017.

THE WORLD IS BETTER WITH

Romance

Harlequin has everything from contemporary, passionate and heartwarming to suspenseful and inspirational stories.

Whatever your mood, we have a romance just for you!

Connect with us to find your next great read, special offers and more.

f /HarlequinBooks

🐦 @HarlequinBooks

www.HarlequinBlog.com

www.Harlequin.com/Newsletters

H HARLEQUIN®

A *Romance* FOR EVERY MOOD™

www.Harlequin.com

HARLEQUIN®

A *Romance* FOR EVERY MOOD™

JUST CAN'T GET ENOUGH?

Join our social communities
and talk to us online.

You will have access to the latest
news on upcoming titles and special
promotions, but most importantly,
you can talk to other fans about your
favorite Harlequin reads.

Harlequin.com/Community

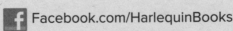

Facebook.com/HarlequinBooks

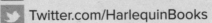

Twitter.com/HarlequinBooks

Pinterest.com/HarlequinBooks